"Ignoring each other isn't going so well for me. How about you?"

"Me either."

Those two simple words powered through him. Eliza was just as drawn to him as he was to her.

Nolan reached out, touching her elbow lightly as snow flurries kept streaming from the sky. "What do you propose we do about that?"

"I have no idea. But I'm open to suggestion."

Exactly what he'd been hoping to hear. "I suggest that we date."

Her eyes went wide in shock. "Date? Like the no-strings sort?"

"Sure. I'm not pushing for a fling," he reassured her. "If you want to go to Moonlight Ridge, we can. But enjoy each other's company while I'm here and agree that we'll say our goodbyes when I leave for home next week."

Even if the thought of those goodbyes already formed a knot in his gut. Yet he couldn't imagine how to keep ignoring the attraction to her. A draw that wouldn't go away.

"That sounds..." Her face smoothed, her eyes searching his for a long moment before she let out a slow breath. "Like an idea worth exploring."

Dear Reader,

Welcome back to Moonlight Ridge, Tennessee, home to the Top Dog Dude Ranch, and thank you for picking up *The Cowgirl and the Country M.D.*! One of the things I'm enjoying most about writing this series is building the community. With each novel, I love the opportunity to "visit" with the friends I've made in prior stories as they support the latest couple on their journey to a "new leash on love."

For this book, a cowgirl stable manager with an equine-therapy specialty brings healing to a widower country M.D. who's got his hands full raising his two young grandchildren. She's no stranger to loss, either. However, thanks to the mischievous kids, puppies, kittens, ponies and even goats, our hero and heroine soon find the famed Top Dog romantic magic has them both smiling. And better yet, has them believing in forever once again.

Just as I enjoy the community of characters in connected stories, I also enjoy the community of readers interacting on social media. Links to my Facebook, Instagram, TikTok and Twitter accounts can be found on my website. Pop in to say howdy and learn more about upcoming Top Dog Dude Ranch novels!

Happy reading,

Cathy

www.CatherineMann.com

The Cowgirl and the Country M.D.

―――――

CATHERINE MANN

HARLEQUIN
SPECIAL
EDITION

ISBN-13: 978-1-335-72422-9

The Cowgirl and the Country M.D.

Harlequin Enterprises ULC
22 Adelaide St. West, 41st Floor
Toronto, Ontario M5H 4E3, Canada
www.Harlequin.com

Printed in U.S.A.

Recycling programs for this product may not exist in your area.

USA TODAY bestselling author **Catherine Mann** has won numerous awards for her novels, including both a prestigious RITA® Award and an *RT Book Reviews* Reviewers' Choice Award. After years of moving around the country bringing up four children, Catherine has settled in her home state of South Carolina, where she's active in animal rescue. For more information, visit her website, catherinemann.com.

Books by Catherine Mann

Harlequin Special Edition

Top Dog Dude Ranch

Last-Chance Marriage Rescue
The Cowboy's Christmas Retreat
Last Chance on Moonlight Ridge
The Little Matchmaker

Harlequin Desire

Alaskan Oil Barons

The Baby Claim
The Double Deal
The Love Child

Texas Cattleman's Club: Houston

Hot Holiday Rancher

Visit the Author Profile page
at Harlequin.com for more titles.

To Mikayla Peeples and Jeanette Vigliotti,
my go-to resources for equine research.
Thank you, ladies!

Prologue

Three months ago; Chattanooga, Tennessee

Goodbyes were hard the first time. But having to say farewell to the same people repeatedly? Agony.

And after losing both her parents within months of each other, Eliza Hubbard was beyond ready for joy.

She shifted her ancient truck into Park and reached for her insulated tumbler, draining the last of her fourth cup of coffee. Sugar had pooled in the bottom, the final gulp sending a much-needed bonus boost of energy surging through her system. It had been a long time since her pumpkin-nut muffin on the run after a morning of mucking out stables before this little road trip to her hometown of Chattanooga.

But she'd made it. And she was that much closer to turning the last page on this chapter of her life. With luck, she would be back in Moonlight Ridge at a reasonable hour.

Exhaling hard, she made fast work of gathering up her leather bag that rested on top of the finalized probate paperwork from her parents' small estate. She was too young to be burying her parents, especially to be handling it all on her own, but she'd been a late-in-life baby and their only child.

Once she finished this trip to clear up her parents' estate, she could move forward. She could put down roots of her own with her new position of stable manager at the Top Dog Dude Ranch. Her dream job. She'd taken the position earlier this year after her parents passed, eager to put the sad memories behind her. But the trips back and forth between Chattanooga and Moonlight Ridge, Tennessee, had been draining.

Thank goodness this was her last stop on her final trip—dropping off a gift to the rehab center. The place had been such a godsend for her parents in maximizing their mobility in their final years. Her dad had been refusing to participate in his PT, until the day the facility had incorporated a therapy dog into the practice.

From that moment on, her father had been all in, a spark of joy lighting his eyes for the first time since he'd started using a walker. The end of his life had been markedly better because of meeting Ozzie, the beautifully gifted golden retriever, and for that Eliza was immeasurably grateful.

Throwing open the door of her pickup truck, the hinges giving a rusty screech, she clutched the gift closer—a bag of homemade dog treats for Ozzie. Her worn boots hitting pavement crunched scattered leaves, the breeze crisp with the kiss of colder weather to come that would call for far more than her jean jacket. She was enjoying the fall weather, but she knew she'd enjoy winter just as much when it came. She loved the outdoors. All seasons, each magnificent in its own way when viewed from the back of a horse.

Her city days were over for good.

She made fast tracks across the parking lot, ready to be back on the road, confident in the skills of the Realtor here who would sell her parents' quaint home where she'd spent most of her life. Even if they got a good price on the house, there wouldn't be much profit after the medical bills were paid, but she only had herself to support, and her new job as stable manager would more than meet her needs. The position even came with an apartment over the barn. Small victories in a year of major losses.

As the automatic doors slid open at the clinic, a wave of memories swept over her. Just as quickly, she pushed them aside. Tried her best to not let her mind catch on the wall-to-ceiling brick fireplace, where her parents had sung Christmas carols with the rest of the patients. Tried her best to put one foot in front of the other on the bright white tiles. She waved to the receptionist behind the sleek semicircular desk. Jade was the heartbeat of this place after working here for decades.

"Eliza, oh my goodness," the receptionist called as she wheeled back her chair and rushed out to wrap her in a hug. "I'm so glad you made it here before my shift ended. I would have stayed longer, though, to say goodbye."

"Aw, I'm so glad to see you, too." She hugged her back hard, Jade's badge digging in. "But please don't let me keep you from work."

The reception area was packed, as always,

with patients ranging from children with crutches to senior citizens with canes and wheelchairs. So many times, she'd sat with her parents at their favorite spot—the gray leatherette sofa by the window—her gaze turned outward toward the mountains, her ears filled with the sound of phones ringing and the crinkle of lozenges being unwrapped.

Stepping back, Jade stuffed her hands into the pockets of her scrubs—butterfly patterned today. "We're at a lull. No worries. And Ozzie will want to see you. He's your biggest fan."

As if on cue, furry yellow dog paws hooked over the half door separating the waiting area from the reception desk. And there was Ozzie peeking over, his golden tail sweeping back and forth. His handler—an occupational therapist in puppy-paw scrubs—was making notes in a file. He smiled quickly. "Hello there, Eliza. Ozzie's on a break. Feel free to give him an ear scratch."

A lump swelled in her throat. Animals like Ozzie were part of why she'd pursed a degree in equine therapy. Eliza reached over to fluff his curly ears. "I already miss all of you so much. I'll be back for more visits." Was she trying to convince them or herself? Hadn't she just been musing on the fact that she was about to be done with city life permanently? "I'm only a few hours away."

The Top Dog Dude Ranch was not far outside of Gatlinburg.

"Honey, this job is your big chance. You were the most devoted daughter I've ever seen—and that's saying a lot." Jade nodded toward the packed waiting room. "You did everything you could for your parents while they were with us, but now that they're gone, it's time to look after yourself, not eat up all your free time coming all the way out here just to pay these old bones a visit. Maybe I'll take a much-needed vacation and come visit you instead."

"I'd love to see you, and I'll make sure they roll out the red carpet for you. As a matter of fact, I have some of the newly printed brochures for the ranch." She fished inside her bag, juggling the dog treats, and found the tri-folded flyer.

Jade plucked one from her hand and read aloud from the first page, "Welcome to Moonlight Ridge, Tennessee—home to the Top Dog Dude Ranch, renowned for family-friendly rustic retreats that heal broken hearts. Some say it's the majestic mountain vistas. Others vow there's magic in the hot springs. All agree, there's something special about the four-legged creatures at

Top Dog Dude Ranch that give guests a 'new leash on love.'" Jade looked up. "Love? For real?"

Eliza nodded, still stroking Ozzie's ears. "From what I've experienced so far? Absolutely. You should have seen the spring wedding extravaganza right after I started working there. So romantic. And this fall, we have all sorts of innovative renovations in the works for family getaways, including accommodations for guests with special needs."

The occupational therapist, a.k.a. Ozzie's handler, popped his head up from the files. "Do you have extra copies of those flyers? I have patients who would probably be interested."

"Of course. Thank you," Eliza said, reaching into her bag again. She pulled out the stack of flyers and placed them on the counter.

Ozzie's nose twitched toward her bag just as the door swept open, inviting in a blast of air along with a man holding a shrieking toddler girl on his hip, her foot in a cast. A young boy trailed behind the pair, his hand gripping the man's jacket.

The girl was screaming, and the boy was tugging the coat so hard it fell down the man's shoulder.

"Mavis, honey, calm down," the man said,

dipping his head toward the girl, snow covering his knit hat. He reached his free hand back for the boy. "Come on, kiddo. We won't be here long, and then we can get a Happy Meal. With nuggets and a toy. Double fries."

Jade reached out. "Dr. Barnett, can I help you with these precious ones?"

The man held up a hand. "Nope. I've got it under control."

Sure didn't seem that way from where Eliza was standing.

In spite of herself, she couldn't look away from the train wreck. But neither could most of the patients in the waiting room, as Eliza's discreet peek around the room showed. Some made a big deal out of focusing on anything other than the man struggling to control his kids, but most were openly staring.

Little Mavis swept her wrist under her nose. "No apples? Okay?"

The man secured his hold on her. "Yes, you can skip the apples."

Jade angled her head toward Eliza, whispering, "Dr. Barnett's a widower. Then his only child died, leaving him the guardian of those two. You wouldn't know it from how he's struggling right now, but he's a very capable man—a country doctor with a thriving practice."

A grandfather?

Eliza's gaze swung back to the broad-shouldered man with the strong jaw. He sure didn't look like any grandpa she'd ever met.

Maybe that was a sign of her own age—her fortieth birthday slipping past her while she'd put everything on hold. Her heart squeezed in her chest. She felt for the guy, understood the strong tug of duty when it came to loved ones.

"That's really sad." Swallowing the lump in her throat, Eliza passed over the bag of treats. "These are for Ozzie. Made fresh by one of the owners of the ranch. Peanut butter pup cakes. I know Ozzie's a big fan of peanut butter."

At the sound of his name, the golden swung his head toward them, his ears perking up. His tail wagged back and forth, fanning fast, stirring a breeze.

Sending the brochures flying off the ledge.

Jade scrambled forward, trying to snag them out of midair. The occupational therapist cued Ozzie to sit before his tail could stir up a tornado.

The stack of papers fluttered, then slapped the ground, fanning outward.

Eliza knelt fast. Only to hit her head on...

The grandpa's head as he leaned down to help her, the thunk softened slightly by his thick knit hat.

"Sorry about that," he said, his voice low and gravelly.

His electric blue eyes held hers. They were so striking that she almost didn't notice the lines of tension crinkling the corners, the smudges of exhaustion underneath.

"Are you okay?" she asked, referring to more than the knock on the head. Knowing she wouldn't get an answer but unable to stop herself from asking the question.

"Some time with an ice pack and I'll be fine. Thanks." He scooped up a flyer.

"Doggie," Mavis chirped, her tears stopping as she reached for the brochure.

The man shot a panicked look Eliza's way. Likely afraid of launching another tantrum if the flyer was taken way.

Eliza smiled. "It's okay. She can keep it. There are plenty more." For good measure, she passed an extra flyer to Mavis, tapping the image of the border collie mix on the front. "That's Loki."

"Loki doggie," Mavis repeated before taking the brochure in her fist.

The man's blue eyes darkened with gratitude as he mouthed the words *Thank you*.

A smile twitched his lips, crinkling up those vibrant eyes framed by dark hair with hints of silver. Somehow, the suggestion of silver made the man's eyes seem even more blue.

Nodding, she resisted the urge to linger. People like this were the reason she loved her job and the Top Dog Dude Ranch's mission: helping the wounded hearts.

And she wasn't interested in losing hers.

Chapter One

Three months later; Moonlight Ridge, Tennessee

Dr. Nolan Barnett had graduated at the top of his class in med school. He'd built a successful practice as a pediatrician.

So how come he couldn't seem to manage all the gear needed to travel with two small children? And who decided to make so many options available for a kid's meal?

Standing at the back of the SUV, snow mixed with sleet pelting him, he looked at the Tetris-like stack of bags and wondered how he was going to unpack it all into the cabin while juggling four-year-old Gus and two-year-old Mavis.

Maybe he'd been overly confident in planning this trip to the Top Dog Dude Ranch. But after he'd found that brochure in the occupational therapist's office back home in Chattanooga, he'd contacted the ranch right away to ask for their first opening. A summer vacation might have been better, with warm weather—less snow and sleet. But the website touted all sorts of kid-friendly winter activities. He'd spent too much of his life waiting for the right time only to lose the chance forever.

So he'd booked the first two-week slot they had available.

Finally, here they were. And no doubt they would need all the healing magic this place advertised sooner rather than later.

The SUV chugged exhaust into the cold air, the heater inside keeping the kids warm and secured in their car seats—devices he found more intricate and dangerous than the procedure to remove an appendix. Leaving the kids buckled in seemed smarter than letting them run in the cabin or even the fenced area while he got everything moved inside. Snow blanketed the A-frame cabin. Trees flanked the structure, their skinny limbs holding heaps of still-piling snow. It was too cold for the kids to run around outside, and heaven only knew what mischief his two grandchildren would get into if he let them play inside unsupervised.

Just this week, Gus had pitched a baseball through the window.

Mavis had dropped the remote control into the fish tank.

Gus had written his name on the wall in permanent marker.

Mavis had covered the bathroom in baby powder, which, when damp, created a paste that lingered for many, many washings.

He knew firsthand.

It would have been funny had his heart not been so broken and his body so weary.

Losing his wife five years ago to an aneurysm had been the worst thing to ever happen to him...until their son, Heath, had died, too, in a boating accident along with Gus and Mavis's mother. Leaving the children with no one else to care for them except for Nolan.

Poor kids. Stuck with a grumpy forty-nine-year-old grandfather in charge of seeing to their every need—as best he could manage.

At the moment, he was feeling more than a bit

inept. No surprise. That was the norm for him since Gus and Mavis had come to live with him six months ago—a transition that had been rocky at best, with every day delivering rougher terrain.

But he was determined to do right by these munchkins. Even if he didn't sleep until he sent Mavis off to college.

Flexing his fingers in the gloves to ward off the cold, he reached inside the SUV for the neon purple bag, a tiara-shaped name tag dangling from the handle. With his other hand, he hefted his own small duffel up and over his shoulder, then grabbed a canvas sack full of "essential" stuffed animals for the children's bedtime.

A quick glance through the SUV's window assured him that Mavis was still snoozing in her puffy pink snowsuit and Gus was coloring with one of those invisible markers that revealed the picture on the page.

Nolan was proud of himself for figuring out that work-around to the wall-coloring issue.

His waterproof hiking boots punched holes in the crusty snow. The place looked idyllic, no question. Clusters of cabins with smoking chimneys were nestled into the mountainside, dotting around the main lodge that sprawled like a rustic mansion. Other guests were out and about, engaged in various activities, echoes of their enthusiasm carrying on the brisk wind. A red barn loomed off to the side along with large stables, riders on horseback in single file on a trail leading into the woods.

This was no small-scale spread. And from what he'd read, it was an expanding operation.

He charged up the steps to the three-bedroom log cabin. A paw-print wreath greeted him with "Barnett Family" stenciled across its center—a part of the package they would be able to take home when they left. He pitched the bags on the porch, and they skidded to a stop by a stone statue of a dog.

Dealing with the day-to-day needs of the kids required more physical labor than he would have ever guessed—from chasing unwilling toddlers through the house for bath time to hauling around all the necessary equipment on outings. He wished he could go back in time and give his wife more credit for all the work he'd left her to shoulder, as Rachel had brought up their son. He hadn't contributed nearly enough time and effort to their family, but she'd never complained. She'd insisted their time would come once he finished med school. When his schedule failed to lighten after that point, she'd started looking ahead to the time they'd have once he'd cemented his place in the practice.

And so on, with one excuse after another keeping him focused on all the wrong things, until too much time had passed and they lost their chance when she died of an aneurysm. He'd found Rachel in their garden, barely alive, draped over her favorite violets with her pupils blown. He'd known even then that there was no hope. And still he'd tried, resuscitating her twice before the ambulance arrived. Hot tears stinging his vision. Shaking hands on her chest. Pleading and bargaining for more time, for a miracle. Only to lose her for good in the emergency room.

His training had failed him when it mattered most. The sight of Rachel's lifeless eyes on what should have been a beautiful Wednesday afternoon never drifted far from his mind.

A thumping sound pulled him back to the present. Gus was pounding his fist on the window.

"Pop! Pop!" His muffled voice drifted out insistently.

Much more of that and Mavis would wake up. Nolan sighed, double timing back, careful of the slick, sleet-covered patches. Reaching the SUV, he opened the door closest to him, adjusting the blanket over Mavis's legs as she stirred, rubbing her eyes.

Nolan whispered to Gus, "I'm here, kiddo."

Gus scrambled out of his car seat and crawled across the floor toward him, half out of the SUV. "Where are the horses? And the doggies? And the cowboys?"

Really? Nolan ground his teeth. "Gus, how did you unbuckle yourself?"

"I've got my Top Dog tag with my name on it. I won't get lost." Gus pitched out of the SUV and into a snowdrift.

Nolan knelt to scoop him up. He hefted Gus up and—

Thump. *Ouch.*

What had thunked into the back of his head?

Clutching a squirming Gus in his arms, Nolan turned too fast...and his boots shot out from under him. He landed flat on his back on the ice. Gus landed on his chest.

Nolan shifted to sit up and set Gus on his feet again...right beside Mavis's pink sippy cup. Which explained the thump on his head.

Sighing, he strained to hold his temper in check and searched for his calmest voice. "Mavis, we don't throw things at people."

"More juice, more juice, more juice." Kicking her booted feet, she patted the cupholder on her car seat.

And tossed two french fries into the snow.

"Do you need some help?" A husky female voice carried on the icy wind.

Startled, Nolan wanted to shout a resounding "yes." He wanted to say that he needed help, and sleep and an afternoon on the sofa watching football. But this trip wasn't about him. It was about spending quality time with his grandchildren and figuring out how to take care of them full-time.

Pushing to his feet, Nolan pivoted to find…

A woman on horseback.

A beautiful woman.

The backdrop of icy trees gave her an otherworldly vibe that momentarily held him motionless. Her caramel-colored braid glistened with frosty snow. An ice-crusted Stetson was perched on her head; she wore a tan jacket with a Sherpa collar flipped up. Her leather boots resting in the stirrups drew his attention to those long, lean legs—something he had no business noticing. She looked confident, bold, stunning.

And she was witness to his ineptitude. Not that it should matter. He wasn't here looking for a hookup. He didn't have an instant to spend on even a passing attraction. Not when there were barely enough hours in the day already for him to keep his family unit functioning. Still, no man enjoyed looking like a fool in front of an attractive woman.

That said, he would absolutely take whatever help she was offering, no matter what the cost to his pride. Otherwise, they might well be out here in the snow until morning. The past few months with the kids had been humbling.

Standing, Nolan drew Gus closer to his leg, gripping a fist full of jacket so the boy couldn't squirm free. "Help? Yes, I need any help you have to spare. As you can see, I've got my hands full with these two."

"Lucky for you, the Top Dog Dude Ranch is full of miracles."

She clicked her brown quarter horse forward, closing the distance between them. Then she swung a leg over and slid down fluidly while Gus leaned closer against his leg, silent for once as he stared in awe at the looming horse.

Reins in her hand, the rider stopped a few inches away. She had green eyes. Beautiful emerald eyes. The color of summer, a surprise in winter, much like the woman.

Something tugged at his memory—a sense of

having seen her before—but he couldn't place where they would have met. No surprise there. His life had been such a blur these past months it was no wonder he could be confused over this woman seeming familiar and also like a stranger all at once.

She had a delicately pointed jaw and freckles across her nose, pretty, but with a hint of steel to her. "I'm Eliza Hubbard. Would you like for me to show the kids how to make snow angels while you get the luggage onto the porch?"

"That would be great." An idea he should have thought of himself. "I'm Nolan Barnett. This is Mavis and that's Gus. I'm sorry to have disrupted your horseback ride. I hope your vacation is off to a better start than mine."

Something like recognition flickered in her gaze, making him question again where he might have seen her before.

"Oh, I'm not a vacationer." She swept aside her braid to reveal the Top Dog logo on her jacket. "I'm the Top Dog Dude Ranch's stable manager."

Gus shifted his stare from the horse to the woman. "I wanna ride."

Nolan secured the boy's hood back on his head. "It's snowing pretty hard today, buddy. I don't think there will be any riding."

His grandson's face scrunched in frustration, and he puffed a hefty, pouty exhale into the late-afternoon air.

Eliza knelt down in front of Gus, reins still clasped in her gloved hand. Her horse chuffed, nudging the back of Eliza's shoulder. "You just got here, and I bet you have lots of unpacking to do. But when you're free later on, you'll be able to come and take a pony ride. We have an indoor arena, like for a rodeo."

"Whoa!" Gus exclaimed, looking around toward the main lodge and barns. "Is that a special place for cowboys to ride?"

"Yes, it is. And for cowgirls, too. Like me." She tapped the brim of her tan-colored Stetson. "Now, do you think you could help me tie my horse's reins to the fence? Then we can make snow angels until all the luggage is unpacked."

Nolan felt a hint of guilt at taking up her time when she likely had other work she needed to be doing. For a second, he thought about how he should tell her he had everything under control now. But she was the one who'd offered, and he just couldn't bring himself to say no. Not when he'd been short on adult conversation for so long. And Gus was happy and under control. Nolan would stand in the snow until he turned into a snowman to extend this moment. "An indoor arena? I didn't see that listed in the flyers."

"It's new. We only just opened the space last week." She angled a smile at Gus as he "helped" her tie the reins to a tree branch. "Be sure to check on your pillows for the cowboy hats—there's one for each of you."

The boy looked at the cabin, then back at Eliza. "Even one for my grandfather?"

"Even one for your grandfather." She pressed against her knee, pushing back to her feet. "Now, let's get to making those snow angels."

Nolan smiled his gratitude, trying to ignore the spark that crackled through the air like a snap of static. A bit painful, but mesmerizing in the way it could sparkle.

When the luggage was all inside—and the front yard was decorated with about a dozen enthusiastically formed snow angels—he approached the woman again. "Thank you again for your help."

"It's no problem. But just so you know, I can also vouch for our childcare services. Our sitters are all experienced and know CPR."

Any other time, depending on childcare would have sounded perfect. But that wasn't his reason for this trip. He stepped back, putting distance between himself and temptation. "I'm sure it's great, but I'm here to spend time with my grand-children."

"Of course." She secured her hat on her head again. "Goodbye, Gus. Bye-bye, Mavis. And Mr. Barnett. It was very nice to meet you. I'm looking forward to seeing you again soon – maybe at the welcome ceremony in the morning? Enjoy your stay here at the Top Dog Dude Ranch."

He watched her mount up again, undeniably interested in spending more time with her, even knowing it couldn't lead anywhere. This vacation was about figuring out how to parent Gus and Mavis. He'd failed at balancing parenthood and a relationship before. And if nothing else, he learned from his mistakes.

So if he was anticipating seeing her again soon…?

His departure date two weeks in the future would keep wayward thoughts in check.

Eliza urged her quarter horse—Cricket—forward. Cricket was her new favorite on the ranch. Spirited. Smart. Eager to learn and with an instinct for empathy that kept her tuned into her rider at all times. Eliza smoothed a hand over her silken neck.

Normally, any time she was on horseback, she

would lose herself in the joy of riding through the snowy sunset after so long living in the city limits, caring for her aging parents. Opportunities for rides on her own had been few and far between giving riding lessons to kids who were only there because their parents forced them. She'd told herself to be grateful for the chance to work with horses at all in a job flexible enough for her to care for her parents. Still, over the years, she'd dreamed of a job like this, of free access to hours in the saddle.

But right now, her thoughts kept scampering back to the encounter with Dr. Nolan Barnett and his incredibly adorable grandchildren.

Cricket's hooves crunched along the snowy path back to the lodge, with signs on tree trunks pointing the way. Not that Eliza or Cricket needed directions back to the stables. Careful hoofbeats on the snow, Cricket avoided icy patches without guidance from Eliza. The mare was intuitive, attentive—which meant that Eliza didn't need to concentrate on the ride and could, instead, let her thoughts wander.

She had seen some unexpected things happen with guests here in Moonlight Ridge, Tennessee. But running across the sexy doctor/grandfather today? That took the cake.

Who would have thought a chance encounter back in Chattanooga three months ago would lead them seeing each other again here, all thanks to a single flyer picked up in passing? It almost seemed as if Ozzie had channeled the Top Dog Dude Ranch magic by sweeping them into Nolan's path at that precise moment. She preferred not to chalk it up to coincidence. Since working here, she'd learned this place and its animals had a special vibe that brought people the healing they needed. She was just thankful to be part of the process with her equine therapy through horses like Cricket.

Speaking of which, she needed to get a move on setting up for tomorrow's grand opening of the indoor arena. The prep would likely drag on long into the night.

As the sun sank farther into the valley, lights along the mountain trail flickered on all the way back to the stables, guiding her path until she reached the indoor arena. The space had been built off the back of the main red barn—a large metal building the size of a gymnasium.

Eliza guided Cricket toward the massive double doors already open, staff rushing in and out on foot and on ATVs with small trailers. Her spirit sang, every breath energizing her. This was her world. Her dream job. And the perfect place to recharge after decades as a caretaker.

To heal after losing her parents.

She led the horse inside, leaving behind the snow-covered ground for a packed dirt floor. The space sprawled in front of her, full of potential. Her mind filled with possibility for making this a go-to place for rodeos. The ranch's owners, Jacob and Hollie O'Brien, had included her in the building plan, spelling out the stages of how they intended to develop it.

For now, it was a multipurpose space, especially useful in the coldest part of winter. Soon, they would add small sections of stadium seating and rodeo stalls. This was a job she could grow far into the future.

Country music piped in softly through the sound system, background noise to the work in progress. The stage was already set up for live music tomorrow. Raise the Woof—a pickup band comprised of members of the ranch staff—would take to the dais. The members of the group changed based on availability, but regardless, the band brought the ranch employees together as surely as any corporate bonding exercise. Eliza joined in on keyboard occasionally, finally putting to use all those hours her mother had made her practice at the piano when she really wanted to be on horseback.

"Eliza, over here." Her boss, Hollie O'Brien, waved, jogging past stalls being set up, a tablet tucked under her arm. She wore a blue flannel shirt and jeans that matched her husband's. They usually coordinated their Western gear as part of the Top Dog Dude Ranch vibe. "You're early. We're not ready to mark off the section for pony rides and the petting zoo."

"I couldn't wait." She swung her leg over before sliding down from Cricket's back and leading the horse alongside as she strode in deeper, eying the double doors at the other end as well that would lead into the barn. "I figured I could take a quick peek now by walking Cricket through to the barn."

"Do you mind if I walk with you? We can talk through tomorrow's event." Hollie tapped a finger along the tablet, scrolling. "If you have suggestions for last minute adjustments, I'm all ears."

The woman juggled life with efficiency and a smile. She and her husband had founded the ranch, building a thriving business and now also parenting their young brood of four children. Eliza was in awe.

Eliza clasped the reins loosely in her hand.

"Whatever I can do to help things go smoothly tomorrow, I'm all in."

"I appreciate your eye for detail." Hollie's gaze slid over to her four children sitting at picnic tables, doing their homework. Tomorrow, those tables would be used for breakfast, featuring baked goods from Hollie's Bone Appétit Café. "It was our lucky day when you accepted our offer."

The timing of the job opening had come less than a month after her parents died. She missed her mom and dad so much she sometimes felt guilty over being so happy here, so fulfilled at the chance to fully utilize her college degree. "I'm thankful you're so open to equine therapy."

"I'm glad to hear you say that, because once we get through the debut of this new space, we want to have a meeting to discuss expanding the program to our other location."

Eliza's clasp on the reins tightened, the outline of the braided leather pressing through her winter riding gloves. The excitement—and pressure—of working here had just increased. This was her chance, and she had to stay focused.

And just that fast, her thoughts trotted right back to her encounter with Nolan Barnett. She cleared her throat. "Sounds amazing. I'm always eager to hear what you have in store for the ranch. And I'm very excited for this new venture. In fact, I would have been here even earlier, but one of our new guests was having trouble settling in."

And how had just a thought of him worked its way into her conversation? She shot a quick glance at her boss, but Hollie looked more concerned than curious.

"Do I need to make a call to the front desk? Is there some problem with the cabin? Did the guest have an issue getting through to someone to help them?" she asked, already tapping along her tablet as they strode past a display from the gift shop that included restored vintage toys and carved wooden animals. "It's been difficult to pace the check-ins today with so many guests battling the weather, showing up at once when the snow slowed. The roads up the mountain are a mess. If this guest called the front desk at the wrong time, I wouldn't be surprised if they had trouble getting someone on the line."

Eliza shook her head. "That wasn't an issue for him. He's a single dad, or rather single grand-dad—" a single, hot granddad "—who was in over his head with two young grandchildren."

"A grandfather bringing his grandkids on vacation?" Her eyebrows shot up. "Alone? That's a new one. Impressive. I try to apprise myself of a brief history on each of the guests before they arrive. Somehow, I got so busy with the renovations I must have missed that detail, because I don't remember seeing anything like that. What's his name? Did you pick up any other information about him that could help us tailor suggestions for his stay here?"

"His name is Nolan Barnett, and as I understand it, he's a widower with custody of the children."

Cricket's nose twitched as they passed the ranch landscaper's booth being loaded with fresh herbs, homemade essential oils and soaps scented with dried flowers. A great perk of working at this place was getting any of the leftovers for free.

There was nothing like sinking into a bath of Epsom salts treated with peppermint oils.

Hollie adjusted a chalkboard easel in front of the display, then said, "Two little ones… I'll make a note for Phoebe from childcare to stop by and introduce herself."

Hollie glanced back at her kids, who'd moved underneath the picnic table with their school supplies. "Mine would be with her now, but Phoebe is interviewing applicants for the new childcare position. Even though our child-to-adult ratio is well within the legal limits, I want even more of a cushion. It's important our younger guests are happily entertained while their parents get a break."

A smile tugged at Eliza's mouth over the memory of the shock on Nolan's handsome face when the toddler had pitched her sippy cup. "He certainly looked like he could use a break."

Steps slowing, Hollie cast a sidelong glance her way. "What *did* he look like?"

Hmm... Now that was a loaded question.

"Young for a grandfather, dark hair, a doctor—" She stopped short, feeling Hollie's knowing gaze. "What? I notice details."

"True. And we love how detail-oriented you are. I was just surprised to see you noticing so much about a *single, male* guest. If something ended up happening there that had you heading back with him to wherever he's from, we'd all be thrilled for you, of course, but we would hate to lose you so soon after finding you. You're irreplaceable." Hollie squeezed her upper arm affectionately.

"Thank you—but rest assured, I'm not going anywhere."

And she meant it. She'd waited too long for this opportunity to sacrifice it. This was her new family. This was the perfect home for her in a rural mountain setting she loved.

So no matter how attractive the sexy grandpa might be, she intended to do everything possible to protect her position at the Top Dog Dude Ranch—and not allow any ideas of romance to get in her way.

Chapter Two

Nolan wondered how he could manage to suture surgical wounds without a second thought and yet couldn't help but fumble his way through securing the rubber bands on Mavis's hair.

How was he still so bad at this? Heaven knew he'd practiced often enough.

Today, his granddaughter sat perched on a bar stool at the end of his first sloppy attempt while he grabbed the brush off the island and started all over again. The scent of java from the coffee maker taunted him with the promise of much-needed caffeine. He welcomed all the help he could get to make it through the day.

He'd reserved this three-bedroom cabin so everyone would have space, only to end up with the kids piling into the room with him. Mavis had said she had bad dreams. Gus said his bed wasn't comfortable. Nolan was very certain that that was not true, but the boy's chin had tipped with bravado that almost hid his fear.

Nolan understood about nightmares and loneliness. And this trip wasn't about him. If climbing in with him made sleeping easier on them, he was more than happy to allow it—even if it meant his own sleep was far from restful.

Thank goodness the kids had slept well for the rest of the night. Now he just had to get everyone dressed and ready in a timely fashion; then the rest of the day should take care of itself, packed with fun—and food—for the kids. Starting with the morning's welcome ceremony the lovely stable manager had told them about.

"Ouch," Mavis cried out, wincing, big tears pooling in the corners of her blue eyes. Blue eyes the same shade as her grandmother's. She would have enjoyed fixing Mavis's hair. Rachel had always wanted a little girl. They had talked about trying for a second pregnancy, but it had just never been the right time to expand their family. Med school. Moves. Rachel's return to college. He'd wanted that for her and was glad they'd made it happen. One less regret.

Nolan cleared his throat, bending closer to console his granddaughter. "I'm trying, kiddo. There are just so many snarls this morning."

A tug on his untucked shirt drew his attention downward. Gus held up a pink spray bottle.

Mavis's detangler.

No wonder brushing was tougher than usual this morning. Nolan had forgotten the bubble-gum-scented leave-in conditioner that would make the work a whole lot easier. "Thanks. You're a smart boy."

"Here's this, too." Passing over a comb, Gus stared up with wide blue eyes too mature for his years. The boy worried so much about his little sister he put his own wants second.

Except for when it came to one thing: Gus insisted on having washable tattoos at all times. Nolan had learned to keep extras on hand for when the current ones wore off. The boy said it reminded him of his mom and dad, who'd gotten tattoos to commemorate their marriage and the birth of each child. The theme behind Gus's tattoos tended to vary. He had been on a super-hero kick last week. This week, he was all about animals.

Nolan took the comb. "Do you want to go pick out your tattoo for the day? I bought some new ones with horses—the pack is on your bed. We have time to put one on before you go."

With a cheer, Gus took off running toward his room—or rather, the room that was supposed to be his. The ranch had personalized the cabin well for their visit.

The main sitting area included two wooden rocking horses, a smaller one with a pink saddle and a larger one for Gus painted blue. A personalized cowboy hat hung from each one.

A massive stone fireplace dominated one wall, but there was a safety screen around it, protecting the children from coming in contact with the hearth. A gift basket full of kid-friendly treats waited on the counter. Cast-iron cookware hung over the stove—not that he intended to do much cooking. He planned to make full use of the ranch's dining hall and any event with meals during the whole two-week vacation. He'd struggled enough with managing groceries and meal planning on his own these last six months. It was tough keeping track of everyone's constantly shifting favorites while avoiding the dishes they wouldn't eat.

Five minutes later—finally—he finished his

granddaughter's hair and stepped back to check his work. Mavis wore her hair in two pigtails. He was getting better at twisting them up into buns on either side of her head like Princess Leia, which was her usual daily style. His daughter-in-law had been a big fan of *Star Wars*.

Gus came running back, a tattoo sticker flapping from his grip. "When are we gonna see the horses?"

Nolan made fast work of putting the small sticker on the top of the boy's hand. "As soon as you put on your coat and boots and gloves."

It wasn't bribery to say that, was it? He didn't think so, anyway.

"I'm trying." He dropped his jacket to the floor and lay on his back, stuffing his arms through. "Can you zip it, please?"

"Of course," Nolan said, impressed yet again by that trick to help a kid pull on their coat. The first time he'd seen it, he'd assumed Gus was throwing his jacket on the ground out of anger, an impression only reinforced when the boy dropped to the floor as well. Nolan had been certain a tantrum wasn't far behind.

Gus tipped his head back as the zipper inched upward. "Will the pretty cowgirl be there today?"

Pretty? Yeah. The kid had good taste.

Coffee. He needed it. Now. "I would imagine so, since she's in charge of the stables."

"What's her name again?" Gus tugged on his stocking cap, pulling it down almost over his eyes.

Nolan adjusted the fit. "Miss…uh, Mrs.… Ms. Hubbard."

He didn't know if she was married or in a relationship. He wasn't even used to thinking about these sorts of things. He'd been devoted to his wife and had never so much as looked at other women while they'd been together. The attraction to Eliza Hubbard yesterday had caught him by surprise.

It still did. So much so that he'd thought about her often during the restless night, until finally he'd placed why her face looked so familiar.

He'd seen her in the occupational therapists office three months ago, when he'd picked up one of the brochures about the Top Dog Dude Ranch. He'd carried the flyer in with him to Mavis's appointment.

"Hey," Gus called, stuffing his hands in his gloves. "Where's my new cowboy hat? I wanna wear it once we're inside and I can take off my stocking cap."

"Cowboy hat. Right." Nolan scratched his

head, trying to remember where he'd put it. Last time he recalled seeing the thing had been when Gus insisted on wearing it after bath time, then climbed onto the wooden rocking horse…

Right. Over there. He rushed to the rocking horses by the fireplace.

Nolan had almost gotten used to how long it took to get out the door with two kids in tow. He regretted all the times he'd sat in the car waiting for Rachel and their son, frustrated because they were going to be late to some event or another. Why hadn't he stayed inside to help her? Or at the very least, listened with more patience and understanding to her breathless explanation when she'd reached the car?

Every day with Gus and Mavis was a crash course in all the ways he'd fallen short at being a husband and a father. But he didn't have time to think about that now. They had an event to attend, and he planned to milk everything he possibly could out of this place in hopes of learning how to do this right. He was determined to go home a better parent figure than he'd arrived.

And what he'd learned so far this morning? Tomorrow, he needed to wake up an hour earlier. And when he woke? He needed to make sure his first thought didn't land on the memory of vibrant green eyes lit with humor he didn't have time to enjoy.

His mind set, Nolan charged into the kitchen and poured an insulated mug full of piping hot coffee, steeling himself for the day.

Morning started early on any ranch, but today had begun even earlier than usual for Eliza. Coffee in hand, she scanned the packed arena, guests already filing in for the morning's event.

Clusters of people crossed from the snowy morning outdoor air into the new building, where the arena was only slightly chilly. A woman about her age held her jacketed arm out for an elderly man to stabilize himself. Even from across the arena, Eliza noted the similarities in their features—the same sharp nose, bright eyes. Her father, she guessed, and a pang rocked through her stomach. Loss remained a material reality in her chest.

Blinking three times to settle the ache inside, Eliza focused on the collective excitement manifesting as smiles and laughter in the crowd.

She'd assigned staff to set up the petting zoo in a corner of the arena and pony rides in the middle with fencing. Later, when the pony rides finished, the fenced-in space would hold a kiddie rodeo, with a horse carousel and wooden ponies to lasso.

The rest of her stable staff would stay in the barn to ensure all the animals were being fed and watered, stalls cleaned. Guests would be moving through the barns as well. She prided herself on making her domain beautiful every day.

But today mattered more than most, and she couldn't afford to be distracted.

She sipped her disposable cup of java. There would be time for a personal life later. Much later.

"Muffin?" Hollie O'Brien sold baked goods along with homemade dog treats, such as pup cakes and peanut butter yogurt, from Bone Appétit Café.

Living here could spoil her, like a working vacation.

"Yes, please." Eliza breathed in the cinnamon scent of the muffin before biting into the topping. "Thank you."

"You're more than welcome. You were here so early I figured you didn't have time to eat breakfast." Hollie nodded a greeting to a couple walking past and gave them a flyer with a listing of all the stalls and events. Her husband, Jacob, stood at the door leading outdoors, welcoming attendees arriving from the other direction. Between them, the indoor arena hummed with life from the rows of booths and events. Raise the Woof crooned a country tune from the dais.

Finishing off her muffin, Eliza tapped against her cup in rhythm with the song, thinking of all the hours she'd spent practicing piano as a child with her mother counting out the beat.

Hollie touched Eliza's arm and whispered, "Is that the single granddaddy you were telling me about? Just behind you?"

Eliza's stomach flipped.

Pivoting on her bootheels, Eliza nearly bumped into Nolan Barnett and his brood. "Uh, hello." When had she turned tongue-tied? "Hollie, this is Dr. Nolan Barnett and his grandchildren, Gus and Mavis."

Hollie smiled, passing over to the children the special booklet full of coloring pages that corresponded with places on the dude ranch. "What beautiful names for beautiful children."

"Family names," Nolan said. He held the little girl on his hip, her hair styled in the most adorable buns on either side of her head.

And the handsome doctor had managed the style? Impressive.

Mavis pulled her thumb out of her mouth.

"Thank you," she said shyly before burying her face in Nolan's neck.

Little Gus shucked his jacket and slammed his cowboy hat on his head, his eyes wide with enthusiasm. "Yep, thanks."

"Be sure to check out the wood carving station, where they can make a puzzle with your name," Hollie said. "Are you finding everything you need to settle in? The ranch prides itself on being family friendly—not just with events but with your whole experience as a visitor, as well."

Nolan set Mavis on her feet, steering her toward the nearby table of carved toys. "Ms. Hubbard was very helpful when I was struggling to wrangle the kids while I unloaded the SUV."

"Eliza's the best. We are lucky to have been able to lure her here. She was in high demand." Hollie adjusted her sleek black Stetson that matched the one worn by her husband.

Eliza's cheeks heated at the praise. She knew how lucky she was to have landed at the Top Dog Dude Ranch. Other organizations may have offered to hire her to fill various roles, but this place was far and above the best suited for her.

Eliza pitched away her coffee cup, focused on making this day a success. Doing her job.

"Is there something else we can help you with, Dr. Barnett?"

"Nolan. Please." He smiled, lines fanning from his blue eyes. "As a matter of fact, we were planning to eat breakfast here, but my granddaughter has dairy allergies. You wouldn't happen to have goat's milk available?"

"We do," Eliza said. "If you'll follow me, I can make sure she has plenty with her breakfast."

Pausing, she gestured for each of the children to pick a wooden toy from a booth just beside the breakfast buffet.

Insulated mug in hand, Nolan strode beside her, his shoulders broad in the tan Sherpa coat, his legs lean in well-worn jeans. "I don't know if you remember me, but we met when you were passing out flyers in Chattanooga."

She angled through the crowd, that day swelling in her memory, the heart-tugging sight of him with the kids, grief wrapping an aura around them. There was still sadness in his eyes, but the children appeared lighter—Mavis "flying" her wooden bird through the air while Gus studied his carved pony.

"I do recall seeing you." She'd wondered, though, if he had remembered as well. "And truth be told, I wasn't there to pass out brochures. I was bringing treats to the therapy dog. The paper storm was an accident—or maybe it was just meant to be."

He laughed softly, a warm sound twining with the sounds of music and other guests. "That explains a lot. I've heard the Top Dog Dude Ranch animals have a bit of magic in them. Apparently, the reach is farther than the ranch boundaries."

"Now, that would be quite a selling point to add to our promotional literature." She waved at the ranch's landscaper at a booth with essential oils and spices, her teenage brother parked beside her, looking less than enthusiastic about spending his Saturday morning at the event.

Nolan scrubbed a hand over his jaw, the stubble appealing. "We were there for PT because my granddaughter has short tendons in her calves that required surgery and therapy."

"Early intervention is key. But then, you already know that since you're a doctor, right?"

"I'm actually a pediatrician with a practice outside of Chattanooga."

She gave a bashful laugh. "Oh, then you *really* know."

"Yes, ma'am." His smile met hers. And held. The corners of that grin slid away even though his gaze did not. There was no mistaking that moment of connection. Of awareness. The crackle in the air between them, a sort of static that popped, lighting the air but with a sting as well. It had been a long while since she'd felt that live-wire of attraction, two years since her last relationship that broke up over her devotion to her parents. He'd wanted her to choose. She'd refused.

A jostle from behind startled her, bringing the world back into focus, the sounds and scents of the welcome event in full swing with food, people and music.

And he seemed as surprised as she was. He blinked fast, like a dazed man coming awake. But it was a fleeting thing. Right?

Dr. Nolan Barnett was a guest here. Even if she were to act on the spark between them, he would be leaving eventually, going back to his practice in Chattanooga. A place she'd eagerly put in her past.

"Excuse me," a hesitant voice called up—Gus, his hands clasped around his wooden horse as he focused blue eyes on her. "After we eat breakfast, are you gonna take us on a pony ride? Pretty please?"

What was happening here?
Nolan couldn't think of worse timing for at-

traction to smack him in the chest. And to make matters more complicated, it appeared there was no way to avoid continuing to spend time with Eliza since his grandson was obsessed with all things horse related.

Of course, she'd said yes to Gus's request. That was her job, after all.

Seated at a picnic table in the arena, he drained another cup of coffee while the kids ate their breakfast. Muffins, monkey bread and fruit cups for the children. They'd even made chocolate goat's milk for Mavis. She was on her second glass, and maybe that was a lot of sugar, but this was a vacation. They were happy and smiling. He couldn't bring himself to say no. He'd promised a pony ride once they finished.

Even considering the pony-ride bribe, he had to admit that the kids were behaving much better than he'd expected. They weren't jumping off their seats, crawling around under the picnic table. They were devouring their meal and playing with their new toys. He realized this pocket of peace was unlikely to last, but he was enjoying the opportunity to bolt down some breakfast of his own—pastries stuffed with cheese and sausage labeled as pigs- and dogs-in-a-blanket.

"Do you mind if I sit here?" a man in a police uniform asked.

Nolan gestured to the open spot across the table. "By all means."

The police officer extended his hand. "Sheriff Winslow."

"Sheriff?" Gus swallowed his food fast. "Where's your star? If you're the sheriff, you should have a star."

The rangy man swung a leg over to sit with his plate of food—two sausage pastries, a zucchini muffin, a banana and pile of strawberries. "It's in my pocket."

"Can I see it?" Gus scooted closer, while Mavis was lost in her own world, feeding muffin crumbs to her wooden bird.

"Sure." The sheriff reached into his pocket, pulled out a leather wallet and flipped it open to reveal the shiny star. "Thanks for the seat. My girlfriend's working a booth, so I'm on my own until she's done...or until I get radioed that someone's stuck in the snow after taking a wrong turn."

Gus slurped his chocolate milk. "Who's your girlfriend?"

Sheriff Winslow nodded toward the landscaper's booth and a woman with a blond braid sporting tiny dried flowers. "Charlotte. She's the pretty lady at the table with all the herbs, essential oils and floral soaps."

Gus frowned, his tongue flicking muffin crumbs from the corners of his mouth. "Mr. Sheriff, how does she grow flowers in the snow?"

Good question, and one Nolan was glad to have someone else on hand to answer. He looked toward the sheriff.

"She has a greenhouse just behind the barn." He patted Mavis on the head gently. "Charlotte even makes scented bubble bath for kids. It doesn't sting your eyes. Or so my girlfriend says."

"Pop doesn't have a girlfriend since our grandma died. I was real little then." Gus stuffed a muffin in his mouth.

Girlfriend? Now, that was a word Nolan hadn't thought about in decades. How surreal to even have it skate through a conversation at this stage in his life. His gaze gravitated back to Eliza Hubbard over by the petting zoo; then he looked back at the sheriff before the man could notice. "I'm just giving my grandchildren a vacation."

"Their parents must be so thankful." Their table partner blew into his coffee, steam rising in the chilly air.

The smile faded from Nolan's face and from the morning. "I'm their guardian."

Music stopped and the sound system squawked as Hollie O'Brien and a man stepped up to the microphone. Thank goodness. Their presence offered a welcome distraction from the sympathy that inevitably flowed from anyone who heard he was the sole provider, the last adult family member, for Gus and Mavis.

The man spoke into the microphone first. "Welcome to the Top Dog Dude Ranch. I'm Jacob, and this is my wife, Hollie." He gestured to the woman in matching Western gear, their shirts black and white checkered, with fringe on the arms. "And these cute rascals are our children—Freddie, Phillip, Elliot and Ivy."

Four elementary-aged children wearing red plaid shirts were perched on the edge of the stage, feet in cowboy boots swinging.

Hollie leaned into the mic. "We founded the Top Dog Dude Ranch with the mission that it would be more than a vacation spot. We wanted to create a haven, a place of refuge with tools available to help enrich your life, ease burdens on your heart, refresh you. It's our hope that you carry a piece of the Top Dog experience with you after your time here is complete."

Jacob continued, "We not only have an amazing staff but the support of our community. Miss

Levine over there—" he gestured toward a young woman in a pioneer costume who was sitting on a rocking chair and holding a scruffy dog "—is a librarian at the local elementary school. Miss Levine helps us with story time here, along with her dog, Atlas. She's offering a very special program over the next two weeks, putting together a theater production with children that acts out the history of Moonlight Ridge. And by 'history,' I mean *the legend*."

*Ooooh*s and *ahhh*s rippled through the crowd, children bouncing up and down in their seats. Nolan knew that the legend had something to do with a lost puppy and a cave, but he wasn't sure of the details. He'd skimmed over that part in the registration material for the ranch. But he could see this was something the kids would enjoy.

Particularly Gus, if there were animals involved. His gaze shot toward Gus, and the boy was bouncing in his seat with excitement.

Would the lovely stable manager be part of the production crew? And why did his mind keep returning to thoughts of her? He really needed to get back to work on his laptop and finish up an article for a medical journal he'd—

That thought stopped him short faster than the one prior. He was here to break the pattern of prioritizing work over the people in his life. Gus and Mavis deserved better than he'd done for their father. His throat clogged with emotion, and he shifted on the wooden seat, needing to gather up his grandchildren, to hug them and let them know they were loved—

A scream split the air. A child's cry. And Nolan's heart fell to his stomach.

Chapter Three

Eliza's heart leapt to her throat as she searched for the source of the childish cry.

She scanned the crowd as a hush fell over the room, heads turning every which way. Eliza peered from the little tykes' rodeo of rocking horses to the picnic tables full of people eating breakfast. Her gaze landed on Nolan and his two grandchildren, and relief coursed through her at the sight of them unharmed and just as surprised by the scream as everyone else. She hadn't even known she was looking for them until that moment.

Still, someone was hurt. But who?

Nolan and Sheriff Winslow stood in unison and moved toward a picnic table across from theirs, where a young couple was kneeling beside a redheaded boy who held a hand against his face, refusing to let anyone look.

Sprinting closer, Eliza called over her shoulder to a stable apprentice, "Get the first aid kit from the tack room." She closed the distance between herself and Nolan. "What's happened?"

The child—probably around eight or nine years old—sat on the floor, rocking back and forth, his parents hovering nervously above while Nolan crouched, assessing.

"This little fella tripped. I'm just trying to get a good look." He reached out a hand behind him. "Some ice in a napkin, please."

Eliza raced to the buffet, scooped up a cup of ice and grabbed a stack of napkins before returning. "Here you go."

"Thank you," Nolan said in a calm voice that gave no hint to any anxiety over the blood oozing from under the boy's hand. "I'm just going to take a peek, buddy, and you can have an icy boo-book bunny. Have you ever had one of those before?"

The child's eyes went wide, and he shook his head. "What's that?"

As he talked, his hand fell away. His parents

winced at the sight of the cut swelling around his mouth.

Clearing his throat, Nolan glanced back over his shoulder quickly, blue eyes brimming with focus. "Eliza, would you mind keeping an eye on Gus and Mavis for just a few minutes?"

All thoughts of keeping her distance vanished. She knew what needed to be done. It only made sense that Nolan would want his grandchildren to be safe and happily distracted from the injury so he could focus on taking care of the boy.

Duty called.

"Of course. We'll get a head start on the pony rides." She turned to the Barnett children. "Would you like that?"

Gus nodded fast, shooting to his feet. Mavis looked back and forth between the horses and her grandfather tending his young patient. Mavis's light blue eyes started to well with tears as she fidgeted with a stray lock of blond hair that had fallen from one of her Princess Leia buns. Eliza didn't want to say the wrong thing that would stress her out or push her over the edge to cry.

Kneeling, Eliza said, "I'll make sure we can see your pop the whole time. And we will get lots of pictures to show him. I bet he joins us really soon."

She hoped she hadn't just lied to the child.

Holding out both her hands, she waited. Gus clasped one first; then finally Mavis slid her fingers into the other in a firm clasp. The pony rides were set up in the fenced-in center of the arena. She led them to the gate and angled inside, stopping in front of the next two ponies waiting to be ridden.

"This is Scooter." She rested a hand on the gelding, a portly dun Welsh Cob pony, then placed her hand on the other, slightly smaller dun Welsh cob gelding. "And this is Clover."

Gus patted Scooter's nose gently. "I wanna ride this one."

"Absolutely." She nodded to a new teen stable hand, who helped the boy saddle up while Eliza kept Mavis tucked safely against her side. "Would you like to ride Clover now? I'll hold on so you don't fall off."

Mavis crossed her arms over her puffy jacket, head shaking. More strands of her hair slipped loose from the haphazard buns on either side. "I want Loki."

Loki? The ranch's border collie? How did she know about...? *Ah.* Then Eliza remembered the day she'd dropped the flyers for the ranch. The one Mavis had picked up had Loki featured prominently on the front. "I'll make sure you get to see Loki after we finish up."

"Promise?" The little girl bit her lip and tilted her head to the side.

"I promise." Easy enough to do. While technically Loki belonged to the ranch since he'd been dumped off as a zany six-month-old, the dog had taken a shine to Eliza when she'd worked on draining his energy by teaching him sheepherding skills. Now Loki spent most of his time either in the stables or in her apartment over the barn. They'd all given up trying to take him back to the lodge where the O'Briens lived—he wanted to be in the thick of the action. "But until then, do you maybe want to try riding on Clover?"

This time, Mavis nodded solemnly.

Eliza grasped the child around the waist and hefted her up, breathing in the scent of baby shampoo and chocolate. Eliza settled Mavis into the special fitted saddle made for a more secure fit for preschoolers.

Clasping the child's hands, Eliza placed them over the saddle horn. "Hold on tight. Now, the next thing we're going to do is get your pony decorated with some beautiful flowers."

Eliza pointed toward the ranch's landscaper, Charlotte Pace, who stood beside a table full of dried flowers and greenery. Some of the flora was loose; other blooms and greenery were woven into wreaths and bows.

Slowly, Eliza walked next to Clover and Scooter. Each pony had a lead line attached to their bridle. Both of these geldings were "bomb-proof"—even-keeled, gentle, not easily spooked.

Charlotte performed a princess wave as they approached. Both ponies knew this routine and patiently paused as the ranch's landscaper approached with her cart full of daisies and sunflowers.

"Welcome, friends. Will you help me pick out which flowers you'd like to be in your pony's manes?" Charlotte spoke in soft tones to Gus and Mavis.

After letting the child select what colors and flowers they wanted, she deftly wove the choices into the thick mane, while additional staff helped with other horses. Mavis chose purple daisies, while Gus selected sunflowers. Charlotte's practiced hands embedded the flower stems into the pony's braided tail itself, securing them with ribbons. She clipped ribbons decorated with dried flowers into Clover's and Scooter's tails.

Eliza glanced back at Nolan, half hoping to catch his electric blue eyes. A circle had gathered around him, but he was so tall she could see the top of his head, his dark hair flecked with silver. He'd placed the child on a picnic table, and he was clearly engrossed in treating the little one. His confidence in his training and experience shone through, and it would be easy to lose herself in staring.

Easy. And reckless. So she pulled her attention back to her place in the world here, where Mavis's high-pitched chatter was a sweet serenade of joy as she prattled to Clover about how pretty she looked.

Some children were already riding in a circle; others were feeding sugar cubes to three extra ponies. This part of her job was the simplest, after so many years giving riding lessons to children and organizing birthday parties for patrons of the stable where she worked. She had always enjoyed the work, but it hadn't been truly fulfilling since there had been few opportunities to share about equine therapy beyond the most basic.

Today's riding was being filmed so later she

could review the footage, assess the riding skills and needs of the younger guests.

Patting Clover lightly on the haunches, she urged the pony forward for her turn getting the floral treatment. Mavis pointed to a wreath of greenery, baby's breath and daisies to add to the other foliage in her ride's mane.

Eliza pointed to a pile of more purple daisies clumped with ribbon. "Would you like some of those to put in your hair as well, to match your pony?"

Mavis nodded eagerly. Eliza reached over to pull two blooms free and clipped them on to each of the Princess Leia buns.

Then the child plucked an extra before reaching for Eliza. "You too."

Smiling, Eliza clipped the bloom into her own hair, just above her ear.

A silver-haired woman dripping in rhinestones and crisp denim leaned on the fence rail, sighing. "My dear, you're a wonderful mother."

Eliza smiled at her, the mistake tweaking an empty place in her heart where she'd once envisioned children of her own.

"Thank you, but they're not mine. I'm just watching them for Dr. Barnett while he looks after the injured boy," Eliza explained, warmed at the compliment all the same. "I work here at the ranch, overseeing the stables." She searched her memory for the woman's name from check-in… Jessica? Jasmine? No. Jacqueline. Jacqueline Tremaine, married to the Tremaine Tire founder.

"Well, you're so good with them." Jacqueline hitched a foot on the lower rung over the railing, her boots pristine with pink paisley stitching. "Are your own children running around here today? They are lucky to have you as their mom."

"Well…" Eliza smiled tightly at the assumption, trying to focus on the fact that it was clearly kindly meant, even if it was rather clueless. She felt a little sting, remembering all the times people had asked her when she planned to settle down and give her parents some grandchildren. Now that wasn't to be for them or for her. She'd dated, sure, and even been engaged once. But in the end, she was on her own. "I don't have any kids. But thanks for the compliment."

Reaching over the rail, Jacqueline patted Eliza's hand. "Well, you look like you still have at least a little time left if you hurry, dear."

Okay, that was a step too far—the touch and the comment. Was she for real? This lady needed a hefty dose of Top Dog magic to cure a toxic case of rudeness. "I don't have one foot in the grave just yet."

"I can't wait to have grandchildren some-day," Jacqueline babbled on, clearly not taking the hint. "But my daughter still hasn't found 'the one.' Hopefully, Top Dog will offer her that re-puted 'new leash on love' while we're here. Per-haps it will give that to you, too."

Eliza bit her tongue. Hard. Counted to ten and reminded herself this was a guest and she couldn't call her out on her impolite statement. For all this woman knew, she had a loving re-lationship with someone already and they'd chosen not to have children. Or *couldn't* have children. In which case, her words would have caused a world of pain. "There are plenty of chil-dren here for me to enjoy—and I don't have to worry about getting up with them in the middle of the night if they're throwing up from eating too much candy."

She softened her words with a smile, but she'd had to say something to put an end to this ex-change.

Jacqueline's eyes went wide as she backed away. "Yes, well, um, I think it's time for my sleigh ride."

Charlotte laughed softly, the blond-haired landscaper tying a bow around the last of the flowers in Clover's flowing mane. "You were far more diplomatic than I would have been. I guess that's why it's a good thing I spend most of my days talking to plants instead."

Eliza put a steadying hand on Mavis's back, sparing a quick look at the girl's grandfather, thinking of him working so hard to bond with the children. "Some of the guests need the Top Dog healing vibe more than others."

"Again, there you are being kinder than I would be." Charlotte nodded to her apprentice and stepped out from behind the table to stand by Eliza. "Do you mind if I walk with you? I need to stretch my legs."

"That would be great. Things have been so busy lately I've missed visiting." She patted Mavis's back, her gaze skating ahead to Gus, who looked at home in the saddle being led by a stable hand. "I do love kids. They're often the most receptive to equine therapy. And I love my job."

"Well, I have my hands full bringing up my teenage brother." Charlotte huffed a blond lock off her forehead, then tucked it behind her ear, her flowered braid beginning to fray. "The last thing I need right now is a child of my own. There's plenty of time for that down the road someday." Charlotte had pale blond hair that many paid top dollar to achieve in a salon. But hers came from hours of outdoor landscaping that gave her natural highlights.

"Your brother is lucky to have you." Eliza understood the call of family obligations well.

Perhaps that's what drew her so to Nolan Barnett—the way he put family first.

Charlotte stuffed her hands in her jacket as she kept stride with Eliza. "Our dad walked out on us right after my brother was born. Mom has mental health issues and is in and out of the hospital. I hope the day comes when she could visit and make use of this place's equine therapy."

Eliza offered an understanding smile. Her own parents had benefited so much from animal therapy. It was a gift, one she was happy to share and pay forward. "I would be honored to help your mother however I can. Your brother, too. He's welcome here anytime. You definitely have a lot on your plate, but you don't have to carry it all alone."

"This job is a godsend." Charlotte swept her boot through the dirt, shuffling aside a loose flower that must have fallen from a pony. "My schedule is flexible so I can be there when my family needs me—and there's no question that my brother and I can use whatever healing TLC the Top Dog Dude Ranch has to spare."

Eliza fiddled with Clover's leather lead, navigating them toward the photographer. Scooter's ears perked forward as they maneuvered around a cone decorated with flowers. Charlotte reached a hand out and stroked Clover's neck as they came to a stop in front of the photographer from their local paper. Milo Clark snapped photos, his graying beard long and knotted in the middle with a leather band. Another cameraman stood to his side, capturing digital footage for Eliza that could also be used in the ranch's promotional material. Hollie was meticulous about checking the guest photo-release forms.

Gus pivoted to look back over his shoulder, glancing at the cameras and then back to her. "Miss Hubbard? Come see me. I'm doing good, right?"

Charlotte nodded. "If you want to go up with him, I can keep watch over this cute poppet."

"Much appreciated," Eliza answered, stepping forward to monitor Gus, relieving the apprentice who'd been walking alongside the boy.

"I've got a horse on my hand." Gus extended his fist, showing her the temporary tattoo, a blue stallion. "You see how the stallion has its hoof up? It's like he is walking. What you can't see in this picture is the frog of the horse's foot. I think they call it that because it's the part of the hoof that looks kind of like a frog if you squint. But also it is really tender, so you have to be careful when you clean the hoof."

Impressed, Eliza steered the horse. No wonder Nolan had chosen this place for the vacation. Gus had clearly read a lot about horses. "What a smart boy you are."

"I wanna be a cowboy when I grow up," he said. He tipped his cowboy hat, wobbled and then grabbed the saddle horn quickly again. "But people keep giving me doctor kits and telling me I can take care of sick people like Pop when I get big."

"That's not a bad thing. But you should also follow your dreams."

"Follow my dreams?" Gus asked, his forehead furrowed in confusion. "But then I would be asleep."

She struggled with how to explain the phrase. "What I meant is that if you want to be a cowboy, then you should work hard and make it happen. Just like I bet your grandfather worked hard to become a doctor."

She scanned the arena, taking in the hum of activity, the echoing whinny of horses. The circle around the injured child was thinning, the boy's mother cradling him while Nolan spoke with them.

He paused before sending a wave and nod of thanks her way. Goodness, but he was too handsome for his own good—and hers.

And given how much Gus loved horses, it appeared she would be spending an inordinate amount of time with Nolan Barnett.

Nolan tossed the paper towels in the trash, his hands cleaned after tending the injured boy. Now to thank the pretty stable manager for her speedy help.

He shouldered through the crowd until he found her by the petting zoo, Gus and Mavis were parked at a craft table, doing some kind of activity with sheep's wool. He allowed himself a moment unobserved to take in the sight of Eliza—her long legs in pale denim, her plaid shirt tucked in, a wide leather belt drawing his attention to her slim hips.

Her fawn-colored hair draped over her shoulder in a low ponytail. A flowered clip hung on for dear life just above her ear. His fingers itched to secure it, to test the texture of her hair, of the pink skin along her cheek.

Clearing his throat, he stepped forward.

"Thank you for keeping such a good watch over Gus and Mavis. I hope I didn't take you from work for too long."

She turned fast, but her footing was sure. "Not at all. It's a part of my job. I'm just glad you were on hand to help with the little boy. How's he doing?"

"It was just a busted lip—he tripped over his untied shoelaces. A dab of antiseptic and a butterfly bandage fixed him right up," he said dismissively. "Anyone could have done the same."

"But the family wouldn't have trusted the advice of just anyone. And it's a half hour to the nearest emergency room. The downside to living on a mountain." She smiled.

He smiled back.

They seemed to do that lots around each other, and it warmed him every time. A jostle against his shoulder brought him back to the present, to the world around them.

"Hello," said a woman with silver hair and over-the-top rhinestone-encrusted Western garb. She shouldered her way between them, inserting herself in the conversation. "I'm Jacqueline Tremaine. Is your nanny taking the morning off, Doctor?"

The way she drew out that last word—*doc-*

tor—was all too familiar. People heard *doctor* and assumed wealth, placing value in that. He just wanted to return to his conversation with Eliza. "This is a family vacation. No nanny."

He turned back to Eliza, hoping the woman would take the hint.

"You came here alone," Jacqueline said with raised eyebrows, the arches painted, "with both kids, without your nanny? Or even some kind of teen sitter? My daughter's here by herself as well, if you need help."

Her daughter? Not a chance.

Nolan looked to Eliza for rescue, but the twinkle in her green eyes indicated how much she was enjoying watching him find his way out of the matchmaker's grip.

"We'll be fine," he assured Jacqueline. "The website said childcare is provided. And the whole purpose of this trip is to strengthen my bond with my grandchildren, so that's really my priority. Nice to meet you."

Clasping Eliza's elbow, he steered her away, moving closer to the children. He tucked his head low and whispered in her ear, "Don't abandon me to her."

Eliza's soft laughter teased his ears. "I can spare another ten minutes to protect your honor."

And before he knew it, they were grinning at each other again. He hadn't smiled this much in—well, a long while.

He looked back at his grandchildren. Mavis was stuffing wool into a cloth toy, and Gus was coloring a paper band for his cowboy hat. "If I'd known this was all it took to make the kids happy, I would have turned the living room into a horse stall."

"That might not be a bad idea."

"My homeowners association would have had something to say about it," he said wryly.

"That's a shame. There's a lot to be said for the therapeutic benefits of riding. I should know— I have a degree in equine therapy." She cast a sideways glance at him. "Though I'll admit, my mother wanted me to be a concert pianist."

He chuckled, thumbs hooked in his jean pockets. "There's not much crossover in those career fields."

"Actually," she said, raising her eyebrows, "there were music majors in some of my psychology classes studying the effect of music on the psyche. Both can have a way of soothing the spirit."

Even as she spoke, her foot tapped in time to the music piping in low over the sound system.

The upbeat tune seemed to have the same effect on others in the crowd—from an older gentleman sweeping his companion into an impromptu two-step to children stomping their tiny boots in time with the beat.

Fascinating. He appreciated a person who challenged him. "Hmm, I hadn't thought of it that way, but it makes sense."

"And I picked up tips on music that helps calm animals. It merges well with the music and art angle that works so beautifully in concert with equine therapy. I told my bosses and they jumped all over the idea. It's one of the things I love most about working here. Hollie and Jacob are always open to new approaches."

"That's a great attribute in a boss—embracing change, empowering the employees." Already, it became clear why the Top Dog Dude Ranch was such a success. Was his ten minutes with her up? He decided to push his luck and try to keep her talking, enjoying the adult conversation. "What did you do before you took this job?"

"After graduation, I worked at a therapeutic riding center for about five years." Her face lit up with excitement, her cheeks flushed.

"And after that?"

A shadow chased across her emerald green

eyes, muting the glow. He would guess whatever came next had not brought her the same joy.

She scratched a fingernail along the metal fencing absently, like a nervous tic. "My parents' health started to fail. I needed to move closer to them and take a job with more flexible hours, so I gave riding lessons to children and I moved back to live at home. My mom and dad didn't have anyone else."

Like how Gus and Mavis only had him.

No doubt Eliza understood the call of family and the need to make the people she loved a priority. From what she'd said about her switch in jobs, it was obvious that she'd taken a position that was far less challenging in order to be there for her ailing parents.

She was a good person. That selflessness was a quality he wanted to emulate.

Yet as he looked from his grandchildren to Eliza and back again, remembering the events of the morning and the boy he'd tended to, he couldn't ignore the sense of déjà vu. Just as he had so often in the past, he'd put family time to the side and gotten absorbed by work.

Logic told him that today was no comparison. There was a world of difference between this and all those years when Heath was a boy and he'd put Rachel in the position of providing all of his care. He was on this trip for his grandchildren, and a few minutes spent dealing with a medical emergency didn't change that.

And this woman wasn't Rachel—wasn't his wife, was barely more than a stranger to him. He wasn't going to forget his boundaries because the day had gotten off to an unexpected start.

All the same, however, his gut warned him to be on his guard and keep his focus firmly on the kids, no matter how many equine events Gus requested.

Chapter Four

Charlotte Pace was hungry. And not for food.

Ducking out of the barn, she stuffed her hands into the sleeves of her parka, trekking through a foot of snow on her way to the greenhouse. Her haven. A landscaper's dream space.

Grow lights hummed overhead, casting a warm glow over rows of flowers and greenery, from lilacs to ferns. From hanging baskets along the rafters to pots in stands. Bundles of drying herbs and blooms hung upside down from hooks.

The scent of earth and plant life soothed her spirit and stirred her creativity.

She made fast tracks past a gurgling fountain built out of a rustic pump flowing into an oversize bucket. She angled by a stack of bagged soil. Finally, she pushed open the screen door separating her office from the rest of the space. Behind her cluttered desk, the wall was full of sketches and plans for future landscape designs at the ranch. Warmth radiated outward as the door swung wide. She blinked, eyes adjusting to the dimmer lighting from the lone window.

Slipping inside, she closed the screen, then pulled the privacy curtain. Heart thudding wildly. Finally, she could snatch a moment just for herself and feed her craving.

Steely strong arms banded around her and pressed her to the desk.

"Hello, beautiful," Declan Winslow growled against her neck. "What took you so long?"

"Does it matter?" she whispered, breathing in the musky scent of his aftershave and gripping the crisp fabric of his uniform.

He was so leanly handsome her teeth hurt. And for now, he was hers.

His mouth found hers, fervent, familiar. Their relationship was only weeks old. Exciting. New. Just for her, at a time of such stress in her life.

Was it any wonder that she gobbled up every moment with him?

His broad palms cradled her face as he kissed her and she kissed him right back, savoring the taste of coffee and Declan. She melted into the feel of him, enjoying the thrill of being in a new relationship—the butterflies, the spontaneity.

Charlotte eased back, her forehead resting against his. Inhaling deep, she drew in the scent of lavender and bergamot, two of the oils that she'd been working with last. An aroma that she knew would forever remind him of her. "I'm glad you could make it here today. Sorry you had to hang out for so long before I could meet with you."

"I'm glad I had the morning free, no emergencies. And it wasn't any hardship to wait. I enjoy this place. It's full of good people." He stroked a finger down the length of her braid. "Like you."

They'd met when he began doing security for larger events at Top Dog. Not that anything untoward had happened here. But the ranch prided itself on safety, and he'd been willing to step in to help. He'd brushed aside any thanks from the O'Briens, saying that he was looking for something to fill his free time between work and the occasional National Guard reserve duty.

She wondered sometimes if the man ever slept—and she had to admit, she would like to watch him sleep. But she couldn't afford to leave her teenage brother unsupervised overnight. The last time she'd stayed out past midnight, Rory had hosted a party at her cabin with over twenty "friends." Her boss had called her, concerned about the noise. Keeping track of him was harder than she'd expected, but he didn't have anyone else since their dad walked out and their mom's mental health deteriorated. There was no telling how long her mother would need treatment.

And Charlotte worried that even when released, her mom wouldn't be up to the challenge of raising Rory.

Sighing, she flattened her palms on Declan's hard muscled chest. "I should get back to work." She patted just over his thudding heart. "Rory can answer basic questions at my booth, but I imagine he's getting antsy. He was not happy about rolling out of bed so early this morning."

"Hold on for just a moment longer." Declan clasped her hands in his, his angular face somber. "Do you know where Rory was last night?"

Unrest swept aside the butterflies. "Studying for a math test and then asleep while I was here setting up."

Silently, he stared back at her intently. Concern etched in the furrows along his forehead.

"No?" she asked with a sinking heart.

All the warmth of the day—the flowers in bloom in her greenhouse and this man's strong arms around her—faded in a flash. A chill took its place.

He shook his head. "There was a break-in at the high school. Nothing was stolen, but graffiti was sprayed on a few walls. There's security footage, and he's on it."

She wasn't even surprised anymore.

Weary, she sank back to sit on her cluttered desk, dried flowers crunching under her and releasing the scent of lavender. "What happens next?"

Declan pivoted to lean a hip on the desk. "He should be okay this time. The video only captured footage of him outside, not actually participating in the vandalism. And the school isn't pressing charges."

It sounded too good to be true. "Why?"

"The mayor's daughter…" he said, his square jaw tight.

"Ah, right." She winced, conflicted on what to do with her brother. It was the question that had plagued their family for most of his life. "It feels wrong to be relieved. He should face consequences. I promise I'll figure out something that'll get through to him."

"I hope so. It's been my experience that small things are only the start."

His words chilled the lingering heat of his kiss and brought her back to the question of how to contain her brother. She had to. For her mom, for her brother and to keep negative blowback from risking her job that was currently supporting her whole family.

She had to keep her brother in line—and, like with their erratic mother, Charlotte suspected it would take every ounce of energy in her already overworked body.

Eliza should be heading to bed now that she'd finished stabling the horses for the night. She'd had the longest of days, and tomorrow didn't promise a light load, either.

She clipped the leash on Loki for a final walk of the evening. A quick walk. Right?

As her feet carried her closer to the lodge, she told herself that her only goal was to take the border collie to see the O'Briens. But she couldn't deny that she looked forward to seeing the Barnett family as they finished up dinner.

Lights shone strategically, illuminating the icy path from the barn.

The lodge was a stately building sprawling with different wings that had been added on to the main cabin as the business expanded. The O'Briens had private quarters in one section, with their own covered porch and gardens. The rest of the massive log building housed guest suites, a dining hall and gathering rooms.

Couples and families ice-skated on the rink out front, the slice of blades and laughter riding the wind. A bonfire flickered off to the side with benched seats all around, where families were roasting marshmallows and singing. A large porch on the side of the lodge sported a bubbling hot tub, currently full of ladies with champagne glasses who'd arranged the trip to help a friend through a divorce.

The air filled with sounds of voices, laughter and camaraderie—the echo of guests relaxing after a day of Top Dog "pack-tivities" ranging from horseback riding and sledding, to quilting squares and spinning wool, to goat yoga and massage therapy.

She appreciated how the ranch incorporated growth moments into those events: quilting patterns reflecting life milestones to celebrate or process; classes making essential oils had an end product that could be used right away in massages to help the participants release tension and get in touch with their bodies; and exercises in team building—so many of those. Everything at the ranch wove through a thread of community.

A dance started in Loki's step as they climbed the stairs toward the main entrance of the lodge. Eliza pushed open the massive wooden door leading into the lobby.

The ceiling soared up to a slanted roof with massive beams. A sprawling antler chandelier hung overhead. The reception desk separated the two areas: one side, a lounging space with massive leather sofas and fat chairs, a large stone fireplace with a roaring blaze.

To the other side, heavy wood tables were used for meals and also for crafting events. A plate of paw-print-shaped cookies rested on each table, with water bottles at every place. Her eyes scanned the room until her gaze found the Barnett family. The children were at a long table with the O'Brien kids while Nolan sat at a nearby table with a laptop and files.

Pausing, she allowed her gaze to linger on him for a moment, taking in all that she admired about him. But she put a time limit on herself. Because she wasn't searching for complications.

But then he looked up in her direction as if aware of her presence. And he smiled. *Oh my.*

It would be rude to walk past.

Securing her grip on Loki's leash, she closed the gap between her and Nolan's table.

As she neared, he stood, holding out a hand for Loki to sniff. "Well, hello. Who's this handsome pup?"

"This is Loki, one of the Top Dog Dude Ranch mascots. He's sort of adopted me." She cued the border collie to lean against Nolan's leg for an ear scratch. "How was your first day?"

He closed his laptop and gestured for her to have a seat. "Easier than yesterday."

"I'm so glad to hear it." She sat, Loki settling under the table at her feet. "Hopefully, tomorrow will be even better. What did you do today after you left the arena?"

"The kids were all about the snow—sledding, snowball fights, snowmen." He leaned back in his chair, long legs stretched in front of him, so close to her that she could feel the heat that radiated off of him even through her jeans. "And Mavis loved the snowshoes that made pretend yeti-monster tracks. What a great activity for her tendons—and much more fun than exercises in a clinical setting."

"That's the hope with what we offer." Was that really her voice? All stilted and formal? "I'm glad she enjoyed herself."

"And if nothing else, the children should sleep better tonight." He scrubbed a hand along the back of his neck for a moment before he rested it on the table. "We're killing time until story hour in front of the fire. The librarian will be reading the tale of the famed legend of Sulis Springs."

"Ah, the magic. I look forward to seeing the children's play on that topic in a couple of weeks."

"I'm just thankful I don't have to sew costumes," he said dryly, spinning his empty water bottle on the table.

"I would imagine you're better at stitching than you give yourself credit for, given all the wounds you've sewn up on kids over the years."

The silence settled between them, charged with that chemistry that she could see was reciprocated. For a moment, she let herself fantasize that they were both guests here, on vacation, free to indulge.

A fun fantasy. But just that.

Scooting her chair back, she snapped her fingers for Loki to join her. "I don't want to keep you. I brought Loki to see Mavis. She asked to meet him, and I promised she could. I'm a woman of my word."

"She'll be thrilled. Thank you."

"Well," she said, feeling awkward and hating that, "I guess I should head over."

"There's no hurry." He touched her elbow lightly. "She's happy having so many kids to play with. If you have the time to stick around...." He snagged one of the unopened water bottles and passed it to her, then nudged the plate of paw-print cookies toward her.

If only it were just the sweets that tempted her.

"I do." She sank back into the chair, picking a cookie with blue sugar sprinkles. "The horses are stabled and fed."

"There are a lot more kids here than I saw this morning." He nodded toward the tables full of children, some of the smaller ones sitting on blankets on the floor for their crafts. "I hadn't expected Gus and Mavis to have this much play-date time."

She grasped the safer, benign subject. Making conversation was easier than wondering why she didn't want to leave. "As Hollie and Jacob said at the welcome ceremony, not all of the children here tonight are guests. Some of these are the families of staff members—including Hollie and Jacob's kids. See the O'Brien children over there? Well, they're with Benji Fuller. He's with Micah, the contractor who's been making expansions to this place. The librarian is his girlfriend. The lady who runs the gift shop is mom to the triplets."

"Triplets? She definitely needs all the help she can get. This place has the best on-site childcare ever. They not only get to use the ranch's daycare but they can bring their kids to events. I need a gig like that," he said with a weary sigh.

And in that moment, she saw him as he was—a guest at the ranch, needing the vacation. Not a fling or even a passing flirtation.

She needed to remember that, remember her position here. "Working here isn't like any other job. We get to experience the magic as well." She scooped up the dog leash. "I truly hope you enjoy your vacation. I'll say hello to Mavis on my way out."

The next afternoon, Nolan was still trying to figure out why Eliza had cut their conversation short at the lodge. He'd enjoyed talking with her. And she was certainly easy on the eyes.

He'd missed adult conversation. Missed having a woman across the table from him.

And before he knew it, he'd arranged with the sitter service to have someone watch over Gus and Mavis while they took their nap to free him up for an afternoon of riding. He had figured if the owners and the staff trusted the childcare here, then he could as well. Especially when they were sleeping.

As much as he wanted his focus on the kids during their vacation, he'd also learned that effective caregiving required breaks. Recharging. Certainly he'd told the parents of his little patients that countless times over the years. He just hadn't realized until recently how difficult it would be to follow his own advice.

Bundled up and ready, he waited at the split-rail fence outside the barn, breathing in the crisp mountain air. Wooded peaks stretched upward, the outside world and worries blocked from view.

Over a dozen guests lined up for their horse assignments, and suddenly he realized Eliza didn't lead all of the trail rides. Jacob O'Brien waited off to the right on a large Tennessee walking horse. Nolan was torn between wanting to spend more time with Eliza and wondering if that kind of distraction was wise. Maybe he should ask to be placed with Jacob.

Then he saw the busybody Jacqueline Tremaine join Jacob's group, along with her husband and daughter.

Nope. Nolan wanted no part of that. Decision made, he hung back, waiting to be in the second group with Eliza.

Finally, she walked his way, leading a Thoroughbred with a reddish-brown mane. Eliza's long caramel braid caught the sunbeams dappling through the icy branches. She wore a wool stocking cap today, tugged over her ears. A paw-print pattern had been knitted along the edges. Her jeans were tucked into her leather boots, a parka cinched in at her slim waist. Her cheeks were pink from the cold, her green eyes reminding him of the promise of spring and life.

Her strength and her confidence were every bit as appealing as her lovely face.

"Good afternoon, Dr. Barnett," Eliza said with a hint of sass in her voice. "Meet Nutmeg. This sweet boy was rescued from a neglect situation and rehabbed here at the Top Dog Dude Ranch."

Nodding his thanks, he took the reins and smoothed a hand along the horse's velvety neck. "Hey there, handsome boy. Ready to show me the sights?"

"We both are." Eliza swung up onto her quarter horse and waved to the group to fall in line, launching into a tour guide speech about the land.

He let her voice wash over him, soaking up the serene beauty around him. Peace was rare in his world lately.

Smoke puffed through the chimneys on cabins and the main lodge. A campground was nestled in a valley, each campsite artfully tucked into the trees, keeping the beautiful integrity of the ranch intact. It was just the kind of place he could imagine enjoying with the kids even more when they were older.

He and Rachel had taken Heath camping, but nothing like this. More of a tent-by-the-water experience. That had been all they could afford during the lean years of medical school.

Nutmeg walked along the trail, sure-footed. Although he noticed Eliza was taking the wider pathway, likely in deference to the snowy conditions, for safety's sake. His gaze skimmed down to the narrow road through the Smoky Mountains leading to the Top Dog Dude Ranch. If this trip had started a day later, they might not have been able to make it up here.

It was like they were sealed off, in a way, from the rest of the world. The scientist in him knew there was nothing magical about that. Just a part of nature. But still, seeing the late-afternoon sunlight glint off the icy branches and snow sure gave the place a mystical effect.

As Eliza paused the trek temporarily to allow riders a chance to dismount and snap photos, he urged his mount alongside hers and said, "Tell me more about the equine-therapy classes for children."

He asked more to make conversation than out of a need to know. He already understood the basics, but he wanted to hear her voice carrying on the quiet afternoon breeze. And yes, to ground himself more in the science of this place and less in the magic.

"The muscles used for gripping the horse, the sense of balance, being in tune with the horse—that's just the tip of the iceberg when it comes to physical benefits a child can gain from horseback riding."

"I had classes on it in medical school and saw workshops on music therapy and pet therapy at conferences. But being here, with the kids?" He teased the reins through his light grip. "It's personal."

"You understand." Her pink lips curved into a beautiful smile, her shoulders relaxing, easing away the formality that had crept between them last night.

"I sure do," he said with a wry chuckle. "I wish I'd understood sooner about a lot of things, though."

"Such as?" she prompted.

"Med school consumed me," he admitted, his confession puffing into the frigid air. Heaven help him, there was something about Eliza that felt effortless. Easy. He knew she could be trusted with this vulnerable truth. He let out a breath. "Not in the normal way. In an obsessive way. I was so afraid of letting down the family tradition, of not finishing at the top of every class, every rotation, that I ended up failing at the most important jobs of all—husband and father."

"Your grandchildren clearly love you," she said, smoothing a leather-gloved hand along Cricket's neck. The horse stretched her neck down, shaking all the way to her withers. "You must have done something right."

But did he deserve that love? Had he earned it? Not yet. "I bought my family expensive gifts to make up for being absent. As if presents could somehow make up for lost time and unspoken words."

"You were trying. I'm sure your son must have seen that."

He hoped so, but he had to accept that he would never know for sure, and that was a heavy weight. Her eyes turned sympathetic, and he was drawn to her. No question. He had been since the first moment he saw her. He just didn't know what to do about it.

A shout split the air, startling him in the saddle.

"Over there!" Jacob hollered. "We need to call back to the lodge for help."

Twisting hard in the saddle, Nolan scanned the horizon until he found a red sedan stuck in a snowdrift. Squinting, he could just barely make out what appeared to be a a driver slumped over the steering wheel. Injured—or worse? Without another thought, he dug his heels into Nutmeg's side, all other thoughts scattering as he focused on what he did best. An arena where he had at least some control.

Leaning low over Nutmeg's neck as the horse took off, Nolan raced toward his patient.

Chapter Five

Eliza dug her heels into Cricket's sides, guiding the horse down the slick, rocking mountainside, following Nolan on Nutmeg.

The moment they had seen the wreck, Jacob had called for an ambulance and began escorting the guests back to the ranch. Once there, he would return with a truck to pull out the car. It would be faster than waiting on a tow.

Hopefully, when she and Nolan got down to the sedan stuck in the drift, the driver would be awake, unharmed other than a bump on the head, in need of nothing more than a tow truck.

Sitting farther into her heels, she adjusted the grip on the reins, slightly tightening her hold to create a more heightened connection between her and Cricket as they carefully picked their way down the stony path. On a summer day, the array of rocks, boulders and ground cover plants would make this descent dangerous.

But in the winter? Eliza drew a sharp inhale of frigid air, carefully working with Cricket to avoid patches of ice. The last thing Jacob needed was two accidents to contend with at the same time. And what would she say to Mavis and Gus if their grandfather got hurt trying to help someone else? Her eyes locked on the red car. Thank goodness for the tree line that had stopped the vehicle from sliding off a cliff. And thank goodness Nolan had arrived on the scene safely. Seeing him take off so fast in snowy conditions had put her heart in her throat as she followed more slowly behind.

Now, as she reached the accident site, she shifted her focus from Nolan to the stranded vehicle. Leaning low on her horse, she angled herself for a better view.

The compact sedan was lodged, nose first, in a snowbank. Two teenage boys were in the front seat: One was passed out behind the wheel, his concert T-shirt soaked from an upended soda. The other whimpered in the passenger-side seat, cradling his arm against his chest, his long dark hair shielding his face.

"Help us. Please, help us," the passenger called, his voice muffled.

"Hang in there," Nolan shouted. "We're here to help. I'm a doctor." Nolan dismounted quickly beside the vehicle and tugged at the door handle, but it didn't budge. He cursed softly under his breath, braced his boots and yanked harder, harder still, until…

The door creaked open a few inches.

Eliza slid down from Cricket and tied both of the horses off to a sturdy branch before picking her way to Nolan.

"Let me help," she offered. Turning, she braced her back against the vehicle and placed one booted foot against the slim wedge of the open door. "I'll push, you pull?"

Nodding, he gripped the edge of the door, stance planted, and pulled while she strained to shove the barrier open with the leverage of her leg muscles. Finally, the door gave way. Eliza thudded onto her bottom in the snow. Scrambling out of the way, she gave Nolan access to the driver.

He leaned in, broad shoulders blocking her line of sight. "Steady pulse. Strong."

Breathing a sigh of relief, she pushed to her feet and brushed the chunks of ice from her pants as she walked toward the front of the vehicle. Through the cracked windshield, she could see the teenage boy in the passenger side.

"Hello!" she shouted. "I'm Eliza from the dude ranch. We've called for help. What's your name?"

"I'm Truett," he said, shivering. "That's my friend Kai. Is he going to be okay?"

Nolan turned on the flashlight feature on his cell phone and pointed it toward Kai's face, lifting one eyelid and then the other. He peered across the driver to his friend. "Pupils are responsive. That's a good sign. How are you doing?"

Truett started to flip his hair back with a flick of his head and winced. "Man, I think I broke my wrist. It hurts. And I can't get out of the car," he said, his voice pitching higher, words piling faster on top of each other. "The trees are blocking my side, and I can't crawl over Kai."

"It's best that you don't move," Nolan cautioned, his words carried on a white cloud puffing into the frosty air. "We need to wait until an ambulance can get here with the proper equipment to remove you. Rushing out can sometimes cause more harm if there's an injury we can't see yet."

Eliza stamped her feet to keep them warm, her legs chilled and a little damp from falling in the snow. "We're going to stay here with you until help arrives. Where are you from? Are you staying at the ranch?"

She didn't think she recognized them from the most current guest roster. But then, sometimes teenagers were tougher to engage in the activities, and parents would frequently let them stay in the cabin rather than argue. And no matter how many times they cautioned guests about the treacherous roads in winter, there were stubborn folks who ventured out beyond their comfort level.

"We're not on vacation. We live in Moonlight Ridge," Truett said, his teeth chattering. "We were just trying to drive up to see our buddy Rory. His sister is the main, like, gardener or something at the ranch. Our parents are going to kill us for being out in this weather. They think we're at the library in town, doing homework. How much longer? I'm freezing my butt off."

Eliza pivoted to the horses and searched through the saddle bags until she found the thin emergency Mylar blankets she always kept there. "This will help keep you and your friend warm while we wait for assistance."

Taking one from her, Nolan's hand bumped hers, his eyes flicking to hers briefly. The moment of connection—awareness, in spite of everything—warmed her inside.

Then, turning back to the boys, Nolan unfurled one blanket open and passed it through to Truett. "Here you go."

Eliza opened the other. "And here's one for Kai as well."

"But what about you guys?" Truett asked, the crinkly blanket held all the way up to his chin. "You've gotta be fr-freezing."

Freezing? Yes. The conditions had worsened since they'd left on their trail ride. And her wet jeans were turning to ice against her legs. But she'd been dressed for cold weather, so at least her coat was warm.

Plus, she wasn't injured, facing the possibility of going into shock. "We're going to be fine." She hoped. "It won't be much longer."

Stepping back, she pulled her phone from the saddle bag and spoke into talk-to-text, unwilling to remove her gloves. "Call Hollie."

The line rang only once.

"Eliza?" Hollie's anxious voice vibrated through the cell. "What's going on with the car?"

"The situation is stable, for now. Is someone on the way with the truck and a winch? We're going to need it. The driver got quite a bump on the head and is still unconscious. There's also a passenger who hurt his arm," she updated quickly, glancing back at Nolan still kneeling by the open car door. "Please say the ambulance is close."

"Yes, to both. Do you know their names?" Worry laced her words even though the noise behind her sounded like business as usual at the ranch. "I've been trying to get in touch with all the guests to see if anyone's missing."

What a nightmare. "Actually, they're a couple of high schoolers from Moonlight Ridge. They were driving up to see Rory Pace."

Hollie exhaled hard. "I feel guilty for being relieved it's none of our guests. I don't know what their parents were thinking, letting them drive with these road conditions. Those two are very lucky your group saw them and that there was a doctor so close by."

Again, Eliza found herself looking back at Nolan—and not just out of worry for the teens but because of her irrepressible attraction to the man. Due to more than just his undeniable good looks. His confidence and calm were mesmerizing.

And she was finding it tougher and tougher to look away.

An hour later, Nolan was cold, tired and so very relieved to be climbing out of Jacob's truck back at the ranch. Even the vehicle's heater hadn't been able to blast enough warmth to cut through the chill that had set in.

By the time the EMTs had arrived, Kai had been awake and lucid. Jacob had arrived shortly thereafter, so Eliza had left, riding Cricket and leading Nutmeg. She'd been a trooper helping with the teens. He'd seen plenty of people panic in times of crisis or opt to stay away from an accident scene all together. But Eliza had been right on his heels to lend a hand, providing quick-thinking assistance.

The EMTs had extricated both teens from the vehicle and taken them to Moonlight Ridge General Hospital for further evaluation.

Jacob had towed the vehicle out of the snowbank so the back end no longer blocked the narrow roadway, moving it to the side of the road to be impounded. Sheriff Winslow was taking care of reporting details of the accident.

Feeling his age, Nolan strode toward the arena, where he'd been told Gus and Mavis were waiting for him. His stomach knotted with worry that they may have missed him or been scared. Jacob had assured him that Hollie had made sure they were well entertained with a group that had story and music time with the small animals. There were even puppies from the local animal shelter to pet.

Gus came barreling out of the double doors, squealing with excitement. Someone had painted a cat on his cheek. "Pop, Pop, you're back. And you're a hero. Everybody says so. You saved their lives."

Nolan knelt, catching his grandson in a hug, relieved to see him so happy. "I just helped them get out of a ditch." He pulled up the hood on the boy's parka. "But thanks, kiddo."

"And everybody's okay?" he asked, his forehead furrowed. Gus buried his face into Nolan's shoulder, his voice small and muffled. "Nobody's gonna die?"

And just that fast, Nolan's relief faded. He stroked his grandson's hair, trying to soothe him. Gus and Mavis had both already experienced too much tragedy for their age. Nolan let out a long, slow exhale. A steadying breath, one he hoped could anchor Gus. "Both of them are fine. They're going to see their doctors, and then their parents are going to take them home."

"But you helped them while they waited. They were safe because you were there." He scooted closer, his arms holding tighter around his grandfather's neck.

"I sure hope so." Standing, he scooped up Gus and started toward the barn to collect Mavis… and make sure she was okay, too. She might be younger than Gus, at an age where experts said she had a better chance of healing faster from the trauma of her parents' deaths, but Nolan needed to see her with his own eyes. Be sure the afternoon hadn't rattled her.

And yes, he wanted to check on Eliza, too.

He thought he caught sight of her in a corral about fifty yards away, giving instructions to two stable staff. She still wore the same outfit from earlier, which worried him. She needed to get into dry clothes in order to truly warm up. They'd sat together in that snowbank during the long wait for help, becoming snow drenched themselves for quite some time.

"I feel safe when you're around," Gus continued, pulling idly at the string on Nolan's hoodie. "I don't get so scared of the dark and being alone."

Nolan's throat went tight with emotion. He swallowed hard before answering, "Glad to hear that. But today was a real team effort."

"With Mr. Jacob and Miss Eliza and all the people here at the ranch? Like how we all worked on the play today during story time?" His face lit up, the solemn mood evaporating as quickly as it had come on. "I'm gonna be a puppy, and Mavis is gonna be a gnome like my new friend Benji."

"Are you happy about that?" he asked, pausing outside the arena door, unwilling to cut this conversation short.

"You bet. I told all the kids we could get sticker tattoos. And we get to start making costumes and paint a… Uh… A mur…" Gus pursed his lips, trying to locate the right word. Annoyance pushed his eyebrows together.

"A mural?"

"Yeah. Miss Charlotte made the paints out of different berries and plants and stuff," Gus explained. "She's a part of our team, too, while we're here. She's a really good helper. I think she should get a sticker."

"It's wonderful to have people in your life to

lean on sometimes." Guilt pinched again over how he'd depended on his wife without giving much in return.

Gus put his hands on either side of Nolan's face. "You can lean on me."

Nolan's heart squeezed hard. "Love you, buddy."

"Love you, too, Pop." Gus rested his head on Nolan's shoulder.

Nolan tried to remember his son at this age, but the demands of residency had been so intense in those days that he'd rarely been home—and when he was, it was usually just to sleep and shower. So much was fuzzy, other than being bone-tired all the time. He pushed the thoughts aside.

Gus started squirming, so Nolan set him back on the ground and took his hand. "Let's go find your sister and have supper."

After he changed into warmer clothes.

He stepped into the arena, lights glowing overhead. The echo of childish play and laughter bounced around the space. The stalls from the previous day's event had been cleared away, but the fencing in the middle remained. A swing set had been erected in one corner alongside a pen of puppies. Another corner had a makeshift movie theater with bench seats and a screen.

Another wall bore a line of playhouses that resembled an old-timey Main Street.

Searching, he found Mavis with the other toddlers in the center fenced-in area, bouncing in an inflatable ball pit. She held up a metallic pink ball in her hand. Even from here, Nolan could hear her distinctive giggle.

Happy. The whole reason for coming here.

He looked down at Gus. "I'm sorry we didn't get to spend more time together today. What would you like to do this evening? Pick anything on the list."

"What about Mavis?" His nose crinkled like he smelled something bad. "I don't wanna always do baby things."

"I'm sure we can work something out."

Gus tapped a finger to his temple. "I know what we can do. There's gonna be a hoedown tonight. My new friends are gonna be there, and we get to go on a hayride behind the tractor."

"That sounds fun." And so much easier than planning activities himself. After this afternoon's unplanned adventure, not having to come up with and execute an itinerary was a real boon.

"There's gonna be music." Gus jumped up and down, his hood flopping back. "Miss Eliza's gonna sing."

And just that fast, his mind filled with the musicality of her voice. A siren's song that, wise or not, he didn't want to miss.

"Grab your partner, do-si-do…"

Eliza played the keyboard as Jacob O'Brien stood on the dais behind the microphone, calling out the dance steps. She was running on fumes, energy wise, but the team was counting on her to play with Raise the Woof for tonight's hoedown.

After finishing up in the stables, she'd raced to her apartment over the barn to change. The hot shower had helped revive her, and the steam eased her scratchy throat, which had been dry from being out in the cold so long. She'd thrown on her ruffled skirt and peasant blouse, then tugged on her matching turquoise boots. She'd grabbed a shawl for good measure to wear indoors in case she got chilled as the evening wore on.

Now, she played the keyboard, the music filling the barn they used for parties and weddings. There weren't as many weddings this time of year, which left the space open.

Her fingers moved deftly across the keys, though she felt as though she was moving through molasses. Gazing around the room, she noted the clusters of tables filled with guests enjoying their meals. Some moved in their seats to the rhythm, letting the magic of music animate their movements.

Tables were set up in the back for meal time. At the Top Dog Dude Ranch, no detail was too small. A decorative wagon wheel created a tiered spread. Jalapeño hush puppies and chili. Hot dogs and potato wedges for pickier eaters. Mini-apple tarts and caramel brownies for dessert.

Pausing between songs, she reached for her thermos of hot tea with honey. The sleepless nights thinking about Nolan Barnett were starting to take their toll. She hadn't had the energy reserves needed to bounce back after the rescue adventure today.

And no doubt, adrenaline from that excitement would have her tossing and turning tonight, no matter how tired she felt.

Jacob leaned toward her, his face gentle, although lines of worry creased his forehead. "You've put in a crazy, long day. We'll be just fine if you want to make a to-go box and head out."

"But there's no one else to play the keyboard," she protested, waving at her station on the stage. Eliza rubbed her eyes, an almost involuntary gesture as she tried to find an untapped well of energy somewhere in her body. Surely she could still rally. "I'm fine."

"They can carry it with the guitars, banjo and drums. The guests will never know the difference." Jacob tipped his Stetson at her.

She held her insulated mug, torn. "Are you sure?"

"Absolutely. You've put in so much overtime we couldn't pay you enough. The least we can do is let you get some rest after an awfully long day."

Nodding her thanks, she turned off her keyboard and made her way down the side steps by the stage. Five minutes later, she had a Styrofoam container of chili and started toward the door, thankful not to have to cook. The food here was incredible. It was another perk of working at the ranch—free room and board.

"Eliza? Eliza Hubbard! Over here."

She searched the crowd, tracing the sound to…two tables away. Her friend Charlotte waved, sitting with her brother, the sheriff…and little Gus seated beside Nolan.

All eyes at the table were on her. Well, all eyes other than Rory's. The teen was texting, only pausing long enough to take bites from a brownie.

But everyone else? They were smiling at her. There was no avoiding them. In particular, there was no dodging that magnetic blue gaze that sent tingles down her spine. Nolan's chambray shirt stretched across his broad shoulders, his hair damp as if he'd recently showered. The thought of Nolan showering sent Eliza's mind reeling, and she struggled not to blush.

Charlotte waved again, gesturing to an empty seat at the table. "Come sit with us. After the day you've had, you should take a load off your feet."

Pivoting toward the group, Eliza approached, telling herself she wouldn't stay long. Whether that was because she didn't want to impose or because she ran the risk of fanning the sparks that ran rampant between her and the sexy doctor, she couldn't be certain.

"Rory," Eliza said, waiting for the teen to look up before continuing, "have you heard anything about how Truett and Kai are doing?"

"They're fine." Rory didn't quite set his phone down, though he did meet her eyes for a moment before he answered in monotone and then returned to his texting.

Grimacing, Charlotte looked at Eliza and mouthed *Sorry.*

"No worries," Eliza reassured her softly, backing away a step. "I'll leave you to your meal."

"Please join us," Charlotte issued the invitation again, patting the empty space beside her on the bench seat. "We would love for you to stay."

Eliza's gaze skipped to Nolan, and he nodded, a smile crinkling the corners of his eyes. Those bright pull-you-into-a-new-orbit eyes.

The sparks flared. Leapt. Proof positive that saying yes would be dangerous.

But how could she say no to her friend?

"All right. I'd love to," Eliza said. Even though she was weary, sitting alone in her apartment didn't sound appealing. Especially with the adrenaline still zinging through her, no matter how tired she felt. She set her thermos and chili on the table and sat by Charlotte, all too aware of the weight of Nolan's gaze. She smiled at Gus. "Are you enjoying your supper?"

The boy nodded eagerly, a napkin tucked into the neck of his sweatshirt. "I ate all my supper, so I get to have an extra brownie. And hot cocoa with whipped cream, even. Why aren't you on stage?" He barely paused for a breath, excitement radiating. "Mavis had to go with the little kids to watch a cartoon, but I got to come here with Pop like a big boy. Are you gonna sing again?"

Words tumbled from the boy's mouth quickly, his feet swinging back and forth faster and faster, bumping the table leg so hard the centerpiece wobbled.

She steadied the arrangement—an upside-down straw hat filled with dried flowers. "I'm done singing tonight. My throat's a bit scratchy."

Nolan's shoulders tensed, his forehead furrowing. "Are you feeling all right?"

"My throat's just a little raw from so long outside today. It's nothing to worry about." She waved aside the concern and pulled the lid off her chili before spooning up a bite.

A hint of heat from the cayenne tingled in her insides, and the warmth of the chili coated her throat. This first bite made her realize how hungry she actually was. She stirred the sour cream and cheddar cheese into the container.

Through her lashes, she looked up at him. "We've imposed on your medical expertise enough already. From now on, you can just enjoy your vacation."

"Uh-huh." Nolan picked up his corn bread and began crumbling it into his chili, fire lighting his gaze. "I'm still going to check in on you tomorrow and make sure you're not pushing yourself too hard."

She noticed it wasn't a question. It sounded more like a promise. And from Charlotte's and

Declan's raised eyebrows and exchange of knowing looks, Eliza wasn't the only one who'd noticed.

Heat stirred inside her, the effects far different from those of the meal.

For a moment, she considered protesting his offer. After so long on her own, viewing herself as a caregiver rather than as someone to be cared for, she wasn't sure what to do with the concern. Or how to take help from others.

Regardless, from the determined look in his eyes, she suspected in this case, she didn't have a choice.

Chapter Six

If a week ago, someone would have told Nolan that he would have time on his hands…

He would have said they were nuts.

But here he stood in the arena, prepping Gus and Mavis for afternoon quiet time after a packed morning. They'd built igloos made of ice blocks that had been dyed different colors. After a change of clothes, they'd moved into the arena for lunch—sandwiches grilled by staff over an electric firepit.

Now they were settling down for their naps in tiny tents erected throughout the arena, each one with a sleep mat and a stuffed Top Dog puppy inside. Children had the option of choosing books to take in with them as well. Soft music piped in through the sound system, slow country tunes.

There were childcare providers posted at every exit, along with nanny cams the parents could log in on for visuals throughout the afternoon.

The kids were taken care of. He could breathe.

"Hello, Dr. Barnett," Hollie said softly, careful not to disturb the little ones just easing off to sleep. While she'd worn Western gear every other time he'd seen her, today she'd opted for a Top Dog Dude Ranch sweatshirt bearing the logo of a horseshoe and paw print. "What are you going to do with your afternoon off? If you don't have plans, we would love to comp you a session with our massage therapist as our thanks for all the help."

"I appreciate the offer." He scratched the back of his neck as he tried to figure out how to discreetly ask for more info on Eliza's whereabouts. "I was thinking of going riding. Aside from the car accident, I enjoyed the time on Nutmeg. Is Eliza leading a group today? I haven't seen her around."

And yes, he was a bit concerned, given she'd noted having a scratchy throat.

Hollie's eyes narrowed suspiciously, and a

smile twitched, but she somehow managed to keep her face otherwise neutral. "Jacob is leading all the trail rides today. Eliza has taken the day off."

He'd expected her to have sniffles, maybe work a half day, but it was clear how much she loved her job, and he couldn't imagine her willingly bowing out for the day. Hearing she had called in sick? Worry knotted in his gut. "How bad is she? It wasn't just cold when we rescued those kids—it was icy and wet."

Hollie nodded. "She sounded pretty hoarse when she called in. I'll admit, I encouraged her to take the whole day off. We want all of our staff to take care of themselves, of course, but she's one of the hardest workers we've ever had. She's more than earned a sick day."

"Is there anything she needs? Anything that I could bring her?" Pressing his hand into his jeans pocket, he tried to channel his professional persona but found a concern seeping through that went a step further.

"Our dining room is sending over meals, and Charlotte dropped off some eucalyptus and peppermint oils to add to Eliza's diffuser. Easy to do, since she lives here in an apartment over the stables."

Well, wasn't that an interesting nugget of information. "That's convenient."

She pulled her cell from the back pocket of her jeans. "Would you like me to phone Jacob and reserve a spot for you in this afternoon's ride?"

Nolan shook his head, scuffing the toe of his boot on the soft dirt of the arena. "No need. I'll just wander out that way and see what pack-tivities pique my interest."

And no doubt, his feet would draw him toward Eliza's place. Had Hollie told him about Eliza's apartment on purpose? Nudging him that way?

"Of course. No need to schedule every minute—vacations are about spontaneity and rest." Hollie stuffed her phone back into her pocket. "Take your time. Once the children wake up from their naps, we're planning a Paws-Up Gymnastics Playtime. Here's a flyer."

"Thank you, ma'am." He scanned the paper covered with cutesy animal-themed clip art with labels like "bear crawl," "giraffe stretch," "ostrich lunge." "Looks like they'll have a blast. I'll be back to collect them by suppertime."

He folded the flyer and tucked it into his jacket. He confirmed his contact information for the childcare service before heading out into the crisp afternoon. Sunshine reflected off the snow.

Not a cloud in the sky.

Of all the events going on today, he could think of only one place he wanted to be. He'd told Eliza yesterday that he would check on her, sure. But what could he do for her beyond that to help her?

A moment later, inspiration struck.

After quick stops at the dining room and greenhouse, he made his way up the outdoor staircase leading to the apartment over the barn.

A railed landing offered a small patio area with two Adirondack chairs and an end table. The doorway held a wreath with Top Dog's horseshoe-paw logo. His heart thudded faster, and he didn't bother deluding himself. He was looking forward to seeing her.

He rapped his knuckles against the wooden panel and waited. If she didn't come right away, he would take it as a sign that she was resting and shouldn't be bothered.

So he waited. And just when he began to turn away, the door swung open.

Oh man. In an instant, he went into doctor mode. Her nose was red, her eyes watery. She was wrapped in a fluffy robe, her hands clutching a fistful of tissues.

She grabbed the edge of the door, Loki nosing up beside her. "Is everything okay? Is something wrong at the ranch?"

"All is well," he rushed to reassure her. He held up a thermos with the special tea he'd put together for her. "I heard you weren't feeling well and thought I would check in. This tea is for you, made special with nettles and mint from Charlotte Pace's greenhouse."

"All natural. I'm impressed," she said with a smile, her voice hoarse. "It appears the Top Dog Dude Ranch way is wearing off on you, Dr. Barnett."

She looked over her shoulder and then back at him, caramel brown hair rippling with the motion, revealing the honey streaks. She bit her lip, head tilting to the side.

"Would you like to come in and keep me and Loki company for a while?" she asked, clutching the thermos to her chest. "We're getting bored in here all alone."

Without hesitation, he knew his answer. "Yes, I would like that very much.

Eliza wanted to attribute her dizziness to her stuffy nose and fever. But she suspected it had more to do with Nolan showing up on her doorstep, and his concern for her. She was touched. So much so, she'd impulsively invited him inside her apartment.

She looked around quickly to make sure the place wasn't messy. Not that she had much square footage to tend to.

The barn apartment sported one bedroom and bath. The rest of the space was devoted to a combo kitchen, dinette and living area. It had come furnished with a cream-colored sectional sofa, a fat comfy chair and a farmhouse table, all in keeping with the ranch's rustic vibe.

A fireplace insert with electric flames heated the room, turned up to high today to ward off the shivers from the annoying chill that had hit her midway through the night. A rumpled blanket was wadded up in the corner of the leather sofa, her tablet discarded after reading had lulled her into a nap.

Nolan's presence in the place made the already compact space shrink even further. She was very aware of him behind her as she walked deeper inside, conscious of his gaze on her—and of her own disheveled appearance. Almost involuntarily, her hand went up to tuck her hair behind her ear. A small attempt to look more put together than she felt as she fought off sickness.

But he was here because he'd heard she wasn't feeling well. She was moved.

Would it be so wrong to indulge in a little time to visit away from all the demands of her work? She tapped the thermos he'd brought. "Thank you for the tea. I hope I'm not keeping you from a pack-tivity with the kids."

"Gus and Mavis are napping under the watchful eye of ranch childcare staff." He shrugged out of his parka and draped it on the antler coatrack on the wall. Eliza noted the line of his strong shoulders even beneath the blue sweater.

"Tent time in the arena?" she asked over her shoulder as she set the thermos on the small kitchen island. Loki's nails clicked on the hardwood floors as he followed her.

"Yes, that's it. Much easier than getting them to settle in the cabin." Nolan's fingers slid along a photo of her parents that rested in a simple gold frame on the end table on his way toward the kitchen island.

She motioned to the ceramic mugs hanging from hooks under the cabinets. "Would you join me in some tea? Or I have coffee already made as well."

"Coffee, if you don't mind. Black. Don't go to any trouble, though, on my account."

She waved aside his concern. "It's the least I can do to thank you for the tea and the house call." She made fast work of pouring steaming drinks for them both. "I've slept most of the day, so I'm wide awake and restless. I appreciate the company."

"How are you feeling? What are your symptoms?" His forehead creased with concern.

She passed him the mug of coffee, then added honey to her tea. Cupping the warmth, she breathed in the minty scent. "Better already, thanks. I'll admit, I felt pretty miserable this morning, but at this point, it's more like a bad case of allergies." She took a sip, the brew soothing her throat. "I expect to be back to work in the morning. If you're sure there's nowhere else you'd rather be, have a seat."

Eliza dropped into the fat leather chair, tucking her feet underneath her and pulling a crocheted blanket over her lap.

"I'm certain." He swept aside a throw pillow and sat on the sofa, taking the corner closet to her on the other side of the end table. "I thought working an eighteen-hour shift at work was rough, but that's nothing compared to keeping up with Gus and Mavis."

Loki jumped up on the couch beside him, snuggling against his thigh.

Lucky dog.

Hauling her attention back to Nolan's face, she said, "While I don't have kids of my own, I can imagine, based on working with children over the years."

"Last month, Gus set up a bowling alley in the living room made out of cans from the pantry. Gus arranged every can of black beans the same distance apart."

"I'm impressed. That's creative." She sipped her tea, eyeing him over the mug.

"He put his sister on a scooter and used her as the bowling ball." He scratched Loki behind the ears, ruffling the border collie's black-and-white fur.

"Ouch." She winced.

"No serious injuries, thank goodness. Just a scraped knee." He crossed one foot over the other, his hiking boots still damp from the snow. "A kiss and a Band-Aid took care of the tears."

"They've been wonderfully well-behaved here." Far better than some others that had come through.

"They're busy. This place may purport having a magical effect, but I fully expect mayhem will return when we get home and get bored again. I'm just hoping to rest up."

Silence settled between them, surprisingly comfortable, especially given how little they knew about each other. She ran her fingers on the rim of her drink. "How long have Gus and Mavis been with you?"

"Six months since their parents died." He looked down at Loki, switching from ear-scratching to smooth petting, as if soothing them both. "My wife passed five years ago."

"I'm sorry," she said softly, reaching across the space to rest her hand on his elbow. While she'd known the basics of his loss, hearing it directly from him tugged at her heart all the more.

Lifting his head again, he smiled, drawing his hand away from the dog. "Enough about that. Let's hit a reset on this conversation. I'm supposed to be making you feel better, not worse."

She considered assuring him she didn't mind hearing about his troubles, but she also had to deal with the grief over her parents in doses, on her own timetable. Perhaps that was true for his grief as well. "Okay. I'm curious. You've said you came to the ranch for Gus and Mavis. But what do you do for yourself—for recreation?"

"I sleep," he said dryly. Loki nudged his hand, urging more affection.

She laughed. "Okay, but what do you do for fun?"

"Nap." His blue eyes were lit with humor, chasing away the somber shadows.

She liked seeing joy on his face and couldn't resist the urge to tease more to the fore. "We need to broaden your horizons. Where would you go for your dream vacation?"

"Hmm…" He quirked a dark eyebrow. "That sounds like a disloyal question, coming from a Top Dog employee."

"You came here for your grandchildren. And there's nothing wrong with that. But I've sat in on enough of the workshops and pack-tivities here to know that the Top Dog mission is about more than your time here. The mission is to effect a change in their guests that they carry forward."

"All right, then…" He nodded, angling closer to her. "Dream vacation… Promise you won't laugh."

"Scout's honor." She placed her hand over her heart.

His eyes lingered there for a moment, bringing heat to her face, until finally, he broke the silence.

"I would like to go to Alaska and stay in one

of those glass igloos where you can see the night sky as you go to sleep."

She couldn't resist tapping his shoulder playfully. "And here we are, back to sleeping again."

"You promised you wouldn't laugh," he reminded her, although there was no sign of anger on his face—just good-natured teasing right back.

"You're right." She inhaled the warm steam of her tea before sipping. "And sleeping under the stars—without freezing—has great merit. Some of our cabins here have skylights. There's even one in the ceiling over my bed—"

As soon as the words left her mouth, she caught herself up short, the implication hanging there in the air between them. Heavy. Enticing. Awareness crackled as tangibly as the electric flames in the fireplace insert.

She cleared her throat, smoothing a hand along the blanket in her lap to distract herself from too-tempting images. "To be clear, that wasn't meant as an invitation." Just knowing it was the right thing to say, the assertion filled her with regret. Still, she forged ahead. "Besides, looks to me like your plate is already full on this vacation."

"Full?" He chuckled lowly, giving Loki a final

pat on the haunches and making Eliza feel grateful that he'd gracefully let her off the hook with the awkward topic. Even if there was still a trace of awareness simmering in his gaze. "My plate is overflowing. And we're right back to the reason napping is my hobby. On that note, I should get back to the kids before they wake up."

She told herself that was just as well, even though she'd enjoyed the time with him.

"Thanks again for the visit and the tea." Setting aside her mug, she stood, drawing the robe closer, realizing with each passing moment that she would need something a lot more substantial than an ugly bathrobe as armor against her growing attraction to Nolan. Less because of his broad shoulders and handsome face and more because of his caring way for everyone around him.

He was a healer—with an overflowing plate.

"Call me if you take a turn for the worse."

"Of course," she lied.

Because no matter the crackling awareness between them, she was fast realizing she and Nolan both had enough loss in their lives. They didn't need to risk bringing on more.

Declan cradled his plate, making his way down the supper buffet, the echoes of bingo calls from across the entry mixing with the clank of silverware in the dining area.

The food at the ranch was always top notch, but he was starting to wonder if he would ever be able to talk Charlotte into a real date downtown. Even though he enjoyed the vacation vibe here, he couldn't forget that for Charlotte, this was like never leaving work. Even now, she'd left her place at the table to answer questions for a couple celebrating their fiftieth anniversary.

Exhaling hard, Declan scooped sautéed Vidalia onions and peppers over his grilled flat-iron steak. Garlic red potatoes, green beans, biscuits and cobbler rounded out the meal. A great meal, but it could have used more of the spice of Charlotte's company.

He just wanted an uneventful evening to chill with his girlfriend – who was finally finishing chatting with the ranch guests.

Joining Charlotte back at their table in a corner purposely chosen for its distance from foot traffic to the buffet, he set down his dishes and pulled her chair out, motioning for her to sit. "M'lady."

"Thank you, Sheriff." She batted her eyelashes at him playfully as she slid into her seat. "Sorry it took me so long to join you."

"No need to apologize. You're well worth the wait." He drank in the sight of her in a flowing brown suede dress and boots, having clearly taken the time to change clothes for their dinner together. "I'm just glad you're here now."

Sighing, she draped her napkin over her lap, then sat up straight again, her eyes scanning the room while concern tightened her normally plump pink lips into a thin line. "Where's Rory?"

"Right over there." Declan pointed toward the dessert table, where the teen was flirting with a high school girl who worked part-time in the gift shop. A rare sighting of Rory without his eyes glued to his phone.

Charlotte smiled apologetically. "I feel like I need to put a tracker on my brother."

"That can be arranged," he said with a wink, half joking. He had a bad feeling about the kid that left him worried for Rory. And for Charlotte.

"No matter what I do, he works his way around it." Shaking her head, a strand of blond hair slid forward over her shoulder. "I have him turn on the locator on his cell phone, and he just leaves his phone in the place he's supposed to be…then uses his burner phone to call his friends when he leaves."

"How did you figure that out?" He reached for the plate of lemon wedges to add to his iced tea as a fiddle player wove around the tables, playing.

"I was doing his laundry, and a burner fell out. I opened it and saw the texting history. I hate being the kind of person who searches a kid's room, but I have to keep him safe."

Charlotte had been thrust into guardianship, and she managed to do all of this for her brother with a smile. She dazzled guests, too. But she seldom got a break—another reason Declan worried for her.

"There were more phones in his room?" He hated the alarms going off in his mind, but he recalled well the lengths he'd gone to as a teen to slip away.

Not to mention all the trouble he'd landed in. He didn't want to assume the worst about Rory, but he also didn't want to miss the signs.

"Two. No drugs, thank goodness. That's what I was really worried about finding." She stabbed at her potatoes, then pushed her plate away. Defeat chased across her face, her eyebrows knitting together. "I feel like even when I succeed in keeping him stapled to my side, it turns out his loser friends are just coming here instead."

"When they're not stuck in a snowbank." The words tumbled out of his mouth, and watching her face fall, he wished he could take them back.

"My brother…" She sighed wearily, nodding toward the doorway, where the teen was trying to duck out with the girl—even though he was grounded. Charlotte shoved back her chair, her good-natured smile returning to brighten her face. "I'll be right back. I'm going to speak with Rory."

She dropped a quick kiss on Declan's mouth before making a beeline toward her brother, her hips twitching with every step. He respected that she took her role as Rory's guardian seriously.

But he also knew this likely meant an end to their date. He returned to the buffet line to get a to-go box for their food. At least that way, she would get something to eat once she hauled Rory back to their cabin.

As he wove around diners in the homey supper hall, he paused at the table where Nolan Barnett sat with his two grandkids in booster chairs.

Declan clapped him on the shoulder. "Hi there. I missed seeing you earlier. I wanted to say thanks again for your help with that car wreck."

Nolan swiped his napkin over his mouth. "I was hanging out with Eliza." He reached over to place Mavis's sippy cup upright again. "She caught a chill from our time out in the snow rescuing those reckless teens."

"How bad?" he asked, his gaze zipping back to Charlotte and her brother, wondering if that kid realized how his actions had affected others. Not likely. "The folks that work here love the job—so much so, it's easy to overdo. Even mealtime is still work."

He nodded toward Charlotte, who was trying to walk back but got stopped by Hollie's assistant. Given the woman was pulling out her tablet, he suspected the conversation could take a while. Declan looked back at Nolan.

"Eliza should recover soon, as long as she rests and takes care of her airways. Hopefully, it won't turn into bronchitis." He grabbed a stack of napkins and mopped up a spill. "Gus, it's okay. We'll get you more milk."

Interesting that the good doc was making house calls. "Well, I won't keep you. You look like you have your hands full."

"That's an understatement." He tossed the milky napkins on his plate of half-eaten steak. "But what can I say? It's all about family time."

The words settled in his gut along with a sense of foreboding. He might not have family, but Charlotte sure did. And if his concerns about Rory proved to be true?

No matter how much he liked Charlotte, he knew where he'd always rate in comparison to her troubled brother. She needed to put Rory first. Given what a mess the kid's life looked like from the outside, Declan had a feeling his relationship with Charlotte would be short lived.

Chapter Seven

Adrenaline sizzled through Eliza's veins as she and Cricket leaned, skirting round the last barrel. Spot on. Tight. She was so focused on her task that she only half registered the sound of Jacob O'Brien's voice over the loudspeaker as he narrated her barrel run. Thank goodness her sore throat had been a short-term thing, because she would have been crushed to miss this.

Now that the arena was complete, mini-rodeos like this one would be a regular occurrence at the Top Dog Dude Ranch, even in winter. The events were open to the public for a small fee—yet another way to increase awareness of the ranch's brand and share their love for the rural way of life with the wider community.

As Eliza gave a light tug to the reins, Cricket slowed from a gallop to a spirited trot. She took a lap around the arena, waving to the folks still cheering for her. Cricket's ears perked forward, and the mare seemed to revel in the spotlight.

Eliza applied a little more pressure on the reins, and her horse began to walk toward the arena's now-open gate. She gave a quick pat to Cricket's damp neck as they moved nearer to the barn. The roar of the crowd dimmed, becoming distant by the time she slid out of the saddle.

Both horse and rider were breathing hard, the adrenaline from before waning. With tired hoofbeats and footfalls, they made their way together to the grand double doors of the state-of-the-art barn. Eliza handed Cricket's reins to the eager stable hand with gorgeous curls and an aptitude for all things equestrian. In the distance, she could just make out Jacob talking the crowd through the transition to the next event: a display of junior roping skills.

Using the free moment to retrieve Loki from a kennel and saddle up on Starlight, Eliza returned to watch the small-scale rodeo's next event. And even though she should have been focused on her upcoming final performance, she scanned the crowd seated on the bleachers lining the arena walls. Searching for Nolan and his grandkids.

Her gaze landed on the trio seated in the middle section, four rows up. Nolan held Mavis on one knee; Gus sat beside him. Both children, wearing cowboy hats and boots, squealed and waved at her. Eliza waved back, a well of emotion catching in her chest at having people in the stands rooting specifically for her.

Standing by her horse and dog, she cleared her throat and thoughts, returning her focus to the ring as time neared for the final event. Loki's moment to shine. Her grip tightened on his leash, the border collie alert at her side as Eliza eyed the end of the junior roping. Little Kacie Archer was a sight to behold. The daughter of the owners of the Top Dog outpost near Nashville, Kacie was a natural. And with parents who were supportive of her rodeo dream, the girl could go far.

Kacie's final toss landed perfectly, and the crowd erupted in response. Everything about Kacie's movements was fluid, ballet-like. Spurred by the crowd, the young girl's face transformed into a wide smile as she took a bow to the sound of thunderous applause. When Kacie stood up straight again, she tossed her straw cowboy hat into the stands before turning on her bootheels and making her way to the barn.

Little Freddie O'Brien, dressed as a rodeo clown, danced for the crowd. He wore an orange wig, his face painted. His baggy overalls were covered in bright patches. With exaggerated antics, he made his way over to the double doors that led into the barn.

Just visible in the closest stall, he gestured to the half dozen sheep.

Loki was laser focused beside Eliza, ready to herd. This was the final event in the little mini-rodeo—and one Eliza was especially proud to have made possible. When she'd arrived here, Loki was a stressed dog searching for an outlet for his energy. Now he had a purpose.

Once the applause died down and Freddie raced back, she unclipped Loki's leash and swung up into the saddle on Starlight. Across the ring, a gate was opened, releasing eight sheep. Eliza dug her heels into Starlight's sides and took off, Loki by her side.

His black ears perked up as he moved toward the three sheep that broke off from the small herd. On quick paws, he collected the sheep, weaving back and forth, gently guiding the wandering sheep back to the other five. From Starlight's back, she could make out Loki's spotted pink tongue as he moved to readjust the littlest sheep that had begun to stray. All around them, the crowd whooped and clapped.

Loki made quick work of clustering the sheep into a tight herd, navigating them toward the open pen, where Freddie hung eagerly on the gate. Continuing weaving behind the sheep, Loki delivered all eight of them into the pen. Freddie closed the gate, cheered, and then took a bow which elicited laughter from the guests.

Peeling away, the dog pranced through the ring, job complete. Eliza slid down from Starlight and walked the horse to the center to join Loki. She gestured to her dog, who deserved his share of the applause.

Jacob's voice chimed through the sound system. "Let's hear it for the star of today's show— Loki!" Applause and cheers swelled through the metal enclosure, up to the rafters. "Thank you, thank you all for joining us today. Be sure to check our website for information on upcoming events."

Reattaching the leash to secure Loki by her side, she returned her attention to the attendees pouring from the stands.

Who was she kidding?

She wanted to turn her attention to Nolan Barnett.

And as if conjured from her wishes, he approached. Mavis in his arms. Gus by his side. Their young blue eyes wide with excitement.

Mavis extended her arms for Eliza.

Nolan tapped Mavis on the chin. "Kiddo, we need to let Miss Eliza get back to work."

"No need to go. I don't mind." Eliza looked from Nolan to Mavis. "Hello, sweetie. Would you like to pet Loki?"

The little girl nodded so hard one of her Princess Leia knots tumbled loose. "Please, Miss Eliza? Please, Pop?"

Nolan's smile was all the encouragement she needed. Eliza held out her arms and gathered up Mavis. The child wrapped her soft arms around Eliza's neck, her hands sticky and precious.

"Loki is also giving out bandannas—you wear it around your neck. Would you like one?" she asked the little girl, who nodded enthusiastically yet again. She helped Mavis pick one out, all the while aware of Nolan's gaze on her.

Once the scarves were chosen and donned by both children, they took turns petting Loki.

Nolan stepped closer, moving out of the way

of a couple angling past as guests and patrons filed out of the arena, the scent of hay and popcorn lingering in the air. "Eliza, you've been so helpful in getting us settled in. I'd like to take you out to dinner on your next day off to thank you."

She froze. Shocked.

Excited.

Eliza struggled for the right words when she really just wanted to cheer. "I wouldn't want to take you from your vacation."

"But would you like to go to a late dinner?" he asked before continuing with a wry grin, "As much as I've enjoyed my time with the kids, I wouldn't mind some adult conversation."

He nodded affectionately toward his two grandchildren with their new best buddy Loki and showing off their bandannas.

"Your offer is tempting." Too much so, especially when she wasn't sure just what this offer meant for her. For him. "I meant it when I said there was no invitation to see my skylight. I don't, uh…get into, uh, relationships with guests."

His eyes went wide. "And I completely heard you. I'm offering nothing more than an invitation to dinner. Truly. I meant no disrespect by my invitation."

The words, his tone, were so gentlemanly, so

earnest. Even a bit old-fashioned. In spite of herself, she was charmed.

And she was swayed. There wasn't a rule against seeing him. She knew of at least one staff member who'd dated a guest and even ended up engaged.

Not that Eliza had any interest in that. Especially not now. "I just wanted to be clear. Because I do enjoy our time together, and I feel guilty about taking you away from Mavis and Gus."

"They'll be asleep most of the time we'll be away. I'll get the kids settled for the night with a sitter after their supper, and then we could go," he said, his eyes on her while his hand rested on top of Mavis's head to keep her from straying. "I heard about this incredible hole-in-the-wall restaurant with all sorts of Tennessee specials."

He seemed to have given this some thought— even done some research into where he could take her. And that nudged her the rest of the way into accepting.

"Well, I do love fried catfish."

His smile dug dimples into his handsome face, which was peppered with a five-o'clock shadow. "I'll take it as a compliment that dinner with me ranks in priority above napping," she teased.

His laughter filled the air and her next breath,

sweeping around inside her and dusting away exhaustion.

She was going on a date.

Two days later, Nolan palmed the base of Eliza's spine as they left the restaurant, stepping into the starry night onto freshly salted pavement that crunched beneath their boots. The touch was born of instinct after their easy conversation over supper. Nothing deep. Just simple and enjoyable in a life that had been far too complicated for a long time.

She was charming and smart. Witty and, yes, beautiful.

They'd lingered over the meal longer than he'd expected. They'd enjoyed dinner on an enclosed back patio with a scenic view of the town's half-frozen river. While the outdoor patio had strategically placed outdoor heaters to ward off the winter chill, he'd insisted on a table by the window instead so she wouldn't risk a relapse of her sore throat.

They'd talked about simple things, like how they'd spent their day—she'd updated records on horses; he'd ice-skated with the kids. Things that made them laugh—she'd played with Loki in the snow; he'd washed marker off Mavis's arms. Books they were reading—she'd devoured a historical romance novel; he'd slowly waded through a medical publication.

Now they settled into an amicable silence, walking side by side. If things had been different, he would have taken her hand or put his arm around her. But he was done wasting time on thinking of what could have been. He was focused on making the most of this moment with this lovely, exciting woman.

Lights illuminated the sidewalk along the main street in the quaint town of Moonlight Ridge. The storefronts were a mixture of Swiss chalet and rustic cabin, with clapboards and A-frame peaks. Window displays showed an assortment of merchandise from gift shops, clothing stores and a couple of cafés—all small scale and quaint. It didn't feel like a kitschy vacation spot but like a cozy, old-fashioned community.

The only nod to the scenic locale? A ski lift for sightseeing over the valley along with transport to a snowboarding hill. The chairlift seemed the perfect way to end the evening.

Main Street was lightly populated, given it was a weeknight during the school year. A half dozen ladies stepped out of a café, each clutching a hardback book and chatting about their book club. Couples and families hurried to their cars, holding shopping bags and doggie bags. People with connections—homes and families and places to go. And for a moment, Nolan felt like life was normal.

Finally, they reached the ski lift launch at the end of Main Street, a small wooden booth at the gate.

He passed his debit card to the teenage girl in the maple booth. Icicles on the overhang glinted. "Two tickets, please."

Smiling wide with a mouth full of braces, the teen handed the tickets over the counter, waving them through. "Enjoy the ride."

"Thank you," Nolan said, his hand on Eliza's back again, the wool of her jacket rasping against his leather gloves.

Twinkling lights along the chairs looked like shooting stars moving toward snow-drenched mountains. Eliza stuffed her hands into her coat jacket as she shivered slightly, making their shoulders brush. They stepped closer, closer—watching as a couple was loaded and launched; then, one after the other, the cars glided along the cable from the cliff over the valley.

Nolan searched her face, looking for any signs

of lingering illness or exhaustion. "Are you warm enough? I wouldn't want you to relapse."

Although she sure looked smoking hot in those black leggings and knee-high boots. Her hair cascaded down her shoulders in loose, spiraling curls that called to his fingers to test. He'd just about swallowed his tongue when he picked her up. His heart rate still hadn't returned to normal.

Eliza shrugged, inching closer to the loading zone, where a man in his twenties explained safety protocol to the couple boarding. "I'm good, thank you. I've got my neck covered, and I'm wearing my hat." She adjusted the fit of the stocking cap, her loose curls flowing down her back. "Honestly, just relaxing is great medicine. I can't believe I haven't taken the ski lift before."

The employee waved them forward. Nolan held his arm out for support as Eliza stepped up and into the open-air cart dangling from a fat cable. Her wide grin sparkled even in the dim lights overhead along the rail.

As the metal car lurched forward, Nolan slid his arm along the back of the seat. "I'm glad we get to experience it together."

And he was glad for the excuse to have her

tucked to his side. Was it his imagination, or did she lean into him?

Eliza's face lit up with excitement as the cart inched along, farther from the mountainside, giving them an overhead perspective of the valley below. "The view of the river is so beautiful from this height." She pointed toward the winding waterway. "You can see it run all the way to the ranch where it feeds into Sulis Springs."

"That's the place with the legend that the kids are doing a play about?"

"Good memory." From above, the metal car groaned slightly on the wire as they climbed toward the mountain. Eliza eyed the steel cable curiously. A slight jerk of the conveyance made her gasp, and she scooted closer. "Tell me more about yourself. You've told me you're a pediatrician, but I don't know much more about your work than that."

Nolan gently rubbed her arm, feeling her heartbeat slow to a normal rhythm, the anxiety of the abrupt swaying receding. "I come from a long line of pediatricians and am a partner in a third-generation family practice outside of Chattanooga."

"Impressive." Eliza tipped her face toward his.

"I'm just a country doctor," he answered, looking into her eyes.

"In a legacy practice," she said, her breath puffing clouds into the night air. "How fulfilling, to live out your dream from the start."

"Truth be told, that wasn't my dream." Those days had been such a blur he'd just forged ahead in the preordained path. "I wanted to be a GP, no pediatrics specialty. But…"

"Family pressure?" she said insightfully.

"I should have pushed harder. It's on me that I gave in." Regrets piled up inside himself. "The worst part is that in chasing their dream, I missed time with my family that I can't get back."

She touched his knee lightly. "If you don't mind my asking, what happened to your wife and your son?"

He understood why she wanted to know, but it was still painful to speak of, so he gave the simplest, barest explanation possible. "Rachel— my wife—suffered an aneurysm five years ago. My son and his wife died in a boating accident six months ago."

Eliza squeezed his knee lightly while empathy knitted her delicate brows together. "That's so much loss for you. I'm sorry."

He nodded his thanks, the weight of her hand

on his knee an unexpected comfort as they sat together, suspended over the rest of the world. He didn't understand why he felt such a connection to this woman he'd known only a short while. But he did. And he wasn't ready for the night to end.

However, he didn't want to spend what time they had left talking about such weighty issues.

Their conversation had grown too somber, with talk of loss. Even knowing this evening together would be a one-off event, he still wanted to make the most of it for her sake as well as for his. To have a happy memory and break from everyday life.

Silence settled between them in the night air, and Eliza wasn't sure what to say. Maybe she shouldn't have asked about his wife. But she was glad to know, all the same.

Now she would let him drive the conversation. It wasn't like she could walk away, given they were locked in a ski lift suspended over Moonlight Ridge's valley.

How had she worked in this area for all these months and not once taken a ride on the open-air lift over the valley? The view from up here was incredible.

Of course, some of the excitement she was feeling could be attributed to the sexy man on the bench seat beside her—so close in the metal enclosure his thigh pressed against hers. His arm extended behind her, and she could swear she felt the heat of it in spite of all the layers between them.

After their encounter when she was sick and in a bulky robe, she'd enjoyed dressing to kill in her favorite thigh-high black leather boots, fleece-lined leggings and long, fitted red sweater.

Thanks to her thick winter socks and parka, she was warm. And happy. Her new hometown was everything she'd hoped for—and yet she hadn't taken the time to explore it beyond a cursory look when she first moved here. Nolan had drawn her out of her comfort zone in a wonderful way.

Nolan's fingers toyed lightly with a loose curl. "Thank you for giving up your evening to come out with me."

"Thank *you* for the evening away from the ranch." A tingle raced up her spine at his touch. "I love the place and enjoy my work, but it's easy to lose track of how long it's been since I left to go anywhere."

"Happy to be of service." His blue eyes twinkled in the moonlight. He kept twining the curl around his finger. "You were something out there with the rodeo this morning."

"What can I say? I enjoy my job." She'd loved rodeo her whole life. "Barrel racing is tame compared to some of the crazy stuff I did back during my teenage years."

"Such as?" He shifted in the seat, rocking the car lightly as he angled toward her, rapt attention on his face.

His genuine interest drew her in. He didn't appear to be asking out of some obligatory politeness like so many others had. She let herself sink into one of her defining memories.

"I had an after-school job at a stable. I was working with a recently gelded horse—Apple—who was really green. Eight years old and he'd never been broken. Naturally, this was just the kind of challenge that fifteen-year-old me wanted." She shot a wry grin his way as she recalled the battle with her mother. "A few weeks in, I clipped a lunge line to Apple's bridle to get him accustomed to the bridle and having a saddle and girth. He started off just fine. Carefully moved through his gaits in the small lunge circle."

Sinking deeper into the story, into the memory, she discovered she could still smell the earth fresh with spring, feel the weight of the line, her every sense finely tuned into training the horse. "Overestimating my skills, I made the very rookie mistake of wrapping the excess lead around my hands—specifically, around my fingers." Her hands fisted inside her mittens at the phantom pain. "He spooked—took off at a gallop across the arena. Because of the way the line was looped…"

Her voice trailed off in a slightly embarrassed laugh. She held up both hands and wiggled her fingers. "He dragged me clear across the arena and broke four of my fingers. My poor mom." Her mother had been in a panic by the time she met Eliza at the emergency room. She'd never said *I told you so*, but Eliza had felt guilty all the same. "Mom wanted a classical pianist daughter. Every event, she was terrified I would break my hand or wrist. Needless to say, Mom's dream for me died that day."

It had taken even longer for her parents to wrap their brain around her drive for rodeo. They didn't truly accept it until her sophomore year in college. Every fiber of her had come alive in just that simple story. It had taken her over two decades, but she was finally living out that passion.

"So, Ms. Rodeo Queen, are there photos of

you? In sequins and fringe?" he asked, a teasing note in his deep voice.

Laughing, she covered her face with her mittened hands. "Sadly, there are quite a few. I made the outfits myself, sewing on the fringe and attaching every sequin. All the way down to the matching bands for the hat and bows for the end of my braids."

"I bet you were stunning." His gaze swept her, all of her.

Her toes curled in her boots. "Let's just say I'm a lot better on the horse than the sewing machine."

"Seems to me like you're a whiz at everything you set your mind to—stable manager, musician, rodeo queen." He counted off the accomplishments one at a time with his gloved hand. "And now master seamstress. I'm impressed."

"Well, for what it's worth, I stink at cooking. The unlimited access to the Top Dog's food services was hugely enticing."

The ski lift paused, hovering, their feet swinging over the craggy valley below, tiny lights dotting the snow-encrusted forest. Beautiful. Remote.

Romantic.

And yes, she felt his gaze on her, holding for

so long there was no doubt that he was seeing her. Just her.

She turned to look at him, truly seeing him in a way that went beyond some superficial noticing. Taking in every line of his handsome face, his square jaw with a five-o'clock shadow, the faint scar in his dark eyebrow. Her hand lifted, skimming over the silver flecks at his temple that only added to his appeal. Attesting to a life lived, survived—experience adding strength of character.

Unable to resist, she angled forward, resting her mouth on his.

Chapter Eight

Nolan had dreamed about having Eliza in his arms, kissing her, and he'd imagined it would be incredible.

But reality far surpassed any fantasies.

Her lips on his. Her soft curves pressed lightly against him. The sweet weight of her arms around his neck. Everything about this moment set his senses on fire.

Nolan slid his hand along the back of Eliza's neck, tunneling his fingers into her loose curls. The glide of her hair over his wrist sent his pulse into overdrive.

The ski lift swayed gently, suspended over

Moonlight Ridge. Up so high, the world was silent, just the two of them. He could near nothing but the sound of her sigh, his own speeding heartbeat.

They seemed to have had all the time in the world to linger in this first kiss, as if time stood still for it. And how surreal to have a "first kiss" at forty-nine; but the surge of excitement sped through him.

Every cell inside him felt alive, soaking in the sensations. The taste of their apple-caramel dessert on her tongue. The silken feel of her cashmere scarf. The crisp winter wind twining around them. Then the ski lift lurched, jostling them closer for a moment, awareness spiking.

But as the gears ground into motion again, the movement brought him back to reality. As much as he would have liked to stay up here longer, to prolong their kiss and this date indefinitely, their time alone was drawing to a close. Tonight had been a one-time encounter. A thank-you dinner. Nothing more. She would return to her job as stable manager, and he would go back to his responsibility to the children.

Regret zinging through him, he eased back, his eyes opening. A fresh wave of desire surged through him at the sight of her, her lips damp and kissed soft. Her eyes were still dazed, and he suspected his were, too. Her caramel brown hair was tousled by the breeze sweeping strands across her face.

Eliza flattened her hand on his chest, her green eyes wide while hints of pink spread across her cheeks. "I'm sorry. I shouldn't have—"

"No need to say anything. It was a memorable moment." Very memorable. One he suspected he would need a long while to process and shake off. "Let's leave it at that."

"Agreed." Her sigh of relief filled the air. "This truly was a wonderful evening out—magical, even. And while I'm grateful for the night away, it's time for us both to get back to our real lives."

Her easy agreement stung more than it should, especially with the sweet taste of her still filling his senses. He suspected that it would be tougher than usual to find sleep tonight.

Because there was no denying that he wanted another kiss—and even more—with Eliza.

The next day, Eliza still hadn't shaken the lingering tingle from her date with Nolan. Hadn't been able to stop thinking of their romantic kiss, suspended above the world in the ski lift.

But she was doing her best to lose herself in her work, reminding her how much she loved the job.

Today, she was leading an equine therapy class geared toward educating children. As always, the experience was moving. They started with pony rides and then shifted to chat time and equine-themed snacks from the "grazing station": "hay bales" made of Rice Krispies Treats and cookies decorated to resemble carrots. Once everyone had gotten their treats, the class headed over to watch a presentation.

A movie screen had been spread across one side of the indoor arena. Children sat on blankets—some with their parents, others being tended to by the ranch's childcare staff.

She'd tried her best to keep her eyes off Nolan, even though her gaze seemed to have a mind of its own, periodically landing on him kneeling behind Gus and Mavis. One look at him and her mind would gravitate right back to their mind-blowing kiss in the ski lift, a lip-lock that had made her feel like a teenager again. It had scrambled her brain, posing a major temptation at a time when she needed to keep her focus on her career, her future.

This, the ranch, was her wheelhouse. And today's session included a special guest—a former

Top Dog guest. A firefighter who'd lost the use of his legs after an accident on the job. Since his initial visit to the ranch, he'd come back twice with his wife. He was even taking riding lessons in his hometown. Today, he'd agreed to talk with the kids about the benefits of the equine therapy he'd experienced.

His personal testimony and slideshow from his riding was a top-notch addition to the class.

Eliza knelt to reach into a small pet carrier behind her and scooped up a tiny tabby kitten— as promised to their guest. The kitten had come from a feral litter that the staff had spent weeks working to socialize. She placed the little purring furball onto the firefighter's lap. "We appreciate your speaking with us today."

"My pleasure," he said, stroking the kitten he'd come to pick up. "And thanks for my new little buddy here. We're naming her Tiger Lily."

Eliza clapped her hands together. "I love it." She turned her attention back to the young audience just finishing their snacks. "Kids, can we all say thanks to our special guest and his new friend Tiger Lily?"

Applause and cheers and *thank-you*s echoed, filling the arena as the children bounced on their bottoms with energy and excitement.

From beyond the thick double doors, a symphony of neighs and whinnies sounded. Something had the horses active; they were so spirited they seemed to be expressing their approval and agreement in concert with the children. Inhaling deeply, Eliza scented the alfalfa bales that were being distributed to the horses.

Eliza closed the pet carrier and tucked it beside the firefighter's wheelchair before returning her attention to the children. "Now, let's see how good of listeners you are. What are some ways equine therapy can help people?"

Marcellus—a little boy with leg braces over his jeans—called out, "When you ride a horse, it can make your legs stronger. Exercise is good for me."

Benji Fuller raised up onto his knees. "The horse doesn't make fun of us if we mess up. So I feel braver."

Pia, a shy elementary-aged girl with her hoodie pulled so far up and over her head that her face was almost covered, rocked forward. "I can be sad around the horse. The horse comforts me."

Gus's hand shot up, a new temporary horse tattoo glistening. "It's really, really relaxing to be outside with horses."

She didn't miss the way Nolan's hand rested

on his grandson's shoulder briefly, the kind of physical positive reinforcement that came naturally to parents.

Pia swept her hoodie off her head, her gaze fixing on Eliza. "No wonder you love your job so much."

"I sure do, Pia." Eliza's heart filled at the answers and enthusiasm that attested to how effective the presentation had been. "Thank you all for those great answers. You're smart listeners."

And yes, she did love her job. Her work with horses had brought her so much stress relief while caring for her parents. It still did as she processed her grief from losing them.

She snuck a quick look at Nolan, thinking of their discussion about his wife dying. It had been five years, but had he dealt with his sorrow? Regardless, he would be going home in less than a week, resuming his busy life.

His kiss would become a memory. That thought shouldn't have felt like a weight around her.

Clearing her throat, she returned her attention to the restless children. "And that's the end of this pack-tivity. Now, you can take your time saying hello to our horses. The people who work here are in red sweatshirts with a big paw print on front.

They can help you feed the horses and answer any questions."

After the kids finished greeting, petting and feeding the horses, there would be a mini-carnival in the arena and barns. Wooden sand-boxes with pans were set up for kids to "mine" for gold nuggets to use for "buying" toys at the wood-carving stand. There would be crafts like painting rocking horses and decorating a stick horse. Games, including cornhole and sack races, would run all afternoon. The center section of the arena would be open for children to ride all sizes of trikes. Eliza was proud of what they were building here, excited to be part of the process.

All around her, children dispersed, moving like a flock of migratory birds. Only two young guests stayed behind: Mavis and Gus. Nolan towered over them as Mavis bounced up and down with excitement.

Nolan had a child on each side, holding his hands. But they were leaning back, tugging, until finally, he knelt until he was eye level with them. "Come on, kiddos. We need to let Miss Eliza get back to work."

Gus stuck out his bottom lip. "But she said we could ask questions."

Eliza strode forward, not bothering to second-guess herself. Answering questions was part of her job, and that was all there was to it—no matter how glad she was to see Nolan, who was looking so handsome in a thick crewneck cable sweater. "Well, hello, Barnett family. What can I help you with?"

Mavis tugged at the hem of Eliza's fleece-lined jean jacket. "You got more kitties?"

"We do. I have one that lives in the barn. Maybe you can come see it?" She looked to Nolan for permission.

Her stomach knotted as she waited for his answer, wanting him to agree more than she should. Hadn't she resolved to keep her distance? And yet the first time Nolan crossed her path, her willpower had crumbled.

He nodded. "Lead the way."

Stomach somersaulting, Eliza walked with her chin slightly raised. She needed to introduce more calm into her stride, more breeze. She led the Barnett family through the length of the stable, letting her fingers trail along wooden plaques with horse-themed quotes as she passed.

"No hour of life is wasted that is spent in the saddle." —Winston Churchill.

"A horse! A horse! My kingdom for a horse!"
—William Shakespeare.

And one of her favorites… "Courage is being scared to death, but saddling up anyway."
—John Wayne.

Their boots softly echoed as they passed Cricket, who stuck her head out of the horse stall and let out a small chuff. Mavis giggled as the next horse, a chestnut gelding, shook his head up and down. With the Barnetts following close behind, Eliza picked her way past the tack room, rounded the corner and popped open the green door to her office.

In the corner behind her desk, she had set up an extra-large pet kennel with the door off. Clean bedding lined the space for the remaining two tabby kittens. Food and water bowls were inside. A litter box was tucked discreetly behind the crate. Soothing music played softly from speakers on her bookshelf.

They were doing well. Sweet and playful, especially considering their rocky start in life. The feral mama cat had been hit by a car six weeks ago. A hiker had stumbled on the three kittens nearby. They'd been close to death, cold and hungry.

It had been touch and go keeping the trio of

kitties alive, then socializing them. The victory was rewarding, though. Staff members had been socializing and feeding them until they were ready for homes. So far, only Tiger Lily had been placed.

Eliza sat on the floor in front of the kennel and invited the children to do the same, all the while aware of Nolan's silent presence as he leaned a hip against her desk. "The kitties are very sweet, but they are young and we don't want to scare them. Give them time to get to know you. I'll hold the kitten, and you can each stroke the kitty very gently. If the little cat arches away, then we will wait awhile and try again. How does that sound?"

Both children nodded. Eliza lifted the more confident of the kittens into her cradled hands, its fur soft, rib cage vibrating with purring.

Carefully, so very carefully, Mavis skimmed one tiny finger along the furry spine. "Is that okay?"

"Perfect," Eliza said. "Did you know when we listen to a cat purring, it can make us feel better?"

Gus scooched closer on his bottom, taking his turn to pet the cat. "Like riding a horse? Or listening to happy music?"

"That's exactly right." Satisfied the kids were

careful and that the kitten was calm, she set the furball in the steady cradle of Gus's hands.

Gus started humming low in a musical mix of a tune and purring, his face happy. His body was more relaxed than she could recall seeing since the boy had arrived, reminding her just how much stress and change he'd coped with in the last year.

A shadow stretched over her just before a hand fell to rest on her shoulder. Nolan's hand. The touch stirred a longing inside her—a yearning to lean into his palm. She glanced back at him, their eyes holding.

"Eliza," he said softly, his gaze grateful. "That's beautiful. Thank you."

There was no question that Nolan had witnessed the transformation in the boy, too.

She reached back to rest her hand on top of his. There was a connection between them. She couldn't deny it. Part of her wondered if they'd met at a different time, what that may have looked like.

But that was an idle thought, a wish that didn't bear thinking about, considering the different paths they were on in life now. Besides, with the fresh reminder of all that the Barnetts had been through already, Eliza needed to remember that their pasts were even more complicated than their present.

Nolan had been restless for the past day since his time in Eliza's office looking at the kittens. All night long, his thoughts had churned with visions of her ease with the children, the beautiful way she came alive with the animals.

By morning, he'd been so amped he had to find a way to work off the energy. Hollie had suggested he book an appointment with the massage therapist, reminding him that he was still entitled to a complimentary session.

While Nolan had appreciated the suggestion, he'd opted for time in the ranch's gym instead since it had a play area for the kids. Lucky for him, Declan Winslow was already there working out, killing time since his girlfriend was running late after being called to a teacher conference at her brother's school.

Nolan climbed onto the treadmill while Declan pumped iron, oddly relieved at finding someone to talk to.

He pressed the start button on the treadmill and adjusted the settings to a brisk walk on a slight incline. Turning his head to the left, he surveyed the large one-room cabin that that been converted to a small gym. There were two other treadmills, two elliptical machines, a healthy variety of free weights and a spin bike. Across from where Declan stood in front of the weights was a juice bar. One corner was devoted to child-care, with a ball pit and a climbing wall.

Declan bent over, executing a dead lift with perfect form. Sweat beaded along his brow and drenched his shirt between his shoulder blades. "What's up with you and Eliza going on a date?"

Phantom memories of her kiss, the taste of her, ricocheted through him.

Nolan stifled a wince and increased the speed on the treadmill, needing more of an outlet for the energy still zinging through him. Taking a deep breath, he shook his head. "It wasn't a date."

Declan looked unconvinced. "Okay. The two of you—just the two of you—went out to dinner away from the ranch and took a romantic moon-lit chairlift ride." He grinned. The sheriff had an unhurried loping way of walking through life that could lure a person into thinking he was on a lunch break, but his keen eyes missed nothing. "But it wasn't a date."

"You're a regular comedian." Nolan upped the resistance on the treadmill, determined to quiet the restlessness buzzing under his skin with this workout. "Just because you're deep in a relationship doesn't mean everyone else is searching."

"I apologize if I stepped on your toes," Declan said, the teasing gone from his tone. It was obvious the apology was genuine.

"No offense taken." It wasn't the sheriff's fault that Nolan was cranky, all twisted up because of a single kiss. Okay, more than a kiss. The woman's mere presence was enough to knock him off his axis. The kiss had just finished the job. "I'm enjoying the vacation at the ranch, but all that 'healing' they talk about in their promo material has stirred up a lot of baggage."

Declan's jaw went tight in a way that seemed to have nothing to do with lifting and everything to do with stress. "The gym is a good place to sweat out tension. Have you tried out the hot springs in the cave?"

"Nah, that's not something I can take the kids to," he said automatically. He already felt guilty enough about going to the gym. Even though it had a play area, he doubted it was as fun for them as most of what the rest of the ranch had to offer. "This trip is supposed to be about Gus and Mavis."

His granddaughter threw balls into the air,

laughing. He hadn't seen his grandkids look so at peace—or full of joy—in far too long. Gus made it to the top of the blue rock wall and let out a small whoop.

Declan nodded toward the play area. "Looks to me like they're having a great time."

Sure. But for how long? He remembered the look of contentment and ease on Gus's face with the kittens, and he wondered how to recreate that back at home on his own. The stress of not being able to provide all the resources the kids needed every day had been a constant worry for months. "Do you have kids?"

"Nope. Never been married, either. I figure the world is better off not having a mini-me raising hell," Declan said darkly, adjusting the weights on his bar to add a new plate on each end.

There seemed to be some history there, but Nolan wasn't one to dig. If the guy wanted to offer it up, he would. "You seem like a pretty upstanding guy. You're the sheriff. And I heard you're in the National Guard, too."

Declan hesitated for so long it seemed he might not respond at all. Finally, he hauled up the bar with such force it pushed the words from his body. "Trying to make amends."

Amends? Nolan understood all about atoning

for past behavior. He just wondered when a person knew they'd reached the goal.

"Seems to me that you're doing a fine job at erasing the past." Nolan just wished he could say the same about himself. And for more than just the children.

As sweat poured down his body from the exertion, he realized his real reason for coming to the gym today hadn't been simply to work Eliza out of his system. It had been more complex than that.

He needed to come up with a way to make amends to her. Because he knew that, in spite of his best intentions, he'd stirred something between them. He'd allowed the heat between them to grow with his attention to her. With his inability to look away whenever she was near. Even though he'd known it would be a bad idea to get involved with anyone right now. He needed to make amends for starting something he wouldn't be able to finish.

Instead of thinking about how to follow up that first incredible kiss they'd shared, he should be concentrating on finding a way for them to move forward separately, without regrets, once he left.

Chapter Nine

Stifling a yawn, Eliza struggled not to sway on her feet. Not because she felt ill, but because she hadn't had even a free minute since she rolled out of bed at four thirty this morning. To stay busy so she wouldn't think of kissing Nolan? Or to possibly run into him if he attended this outing with Mavis and Gus?

She told herself that the former was the reason behind her actions. But she still suspected the latter.

Now she was volunteering her lunch hour to help with a baking event at the Bone Appétit Café. Solid plan, given she'd heard that the Barnetts would be tubing in the snow for the afternoon.

She'd heard wrong.

They were seated at a back table with a mother and her daughter—little Pia?—looking cozy and laughing together as the children smeared frosting over cookies. Puffy jackets and mittens hung to their left, evidence of the deep chill that had swept through Top Dog Dude Ranch this morning.

A hint of jealousy pinched her, even though Eliza knew she had no right to feel that way. Her fingers worked on the inside of her sweater sleeve, stroking the soft fibers along her wrist, where no one would see the gesture—a moment of self-soothing before the lock she had on her composure became as slippery as the ice shining just outside the large window.

She forced her attention back to the presentation in progress, all the while passing over ingredients like a good "sous chef" to Hollie O'Brien. Today, Hollie was leading the sensory cooking class for her young guests. Bone Appétit Café was the woman's domain, her special corner of the Top Dog Dude Ranch. The quaint café was brightly lit and filled with ice cream parlor style tables and chairs, surrounded by walls brimming with chocolates and baked goods. Warm yellow lights made the space cozier, homey.

There were two sides to the shop: one for

human treats and one for pooch treats. Ice cream. Cakes. Cookies. All filling the air with the scent of vanilla, cinnamon and chocolate.

Today, the children were making animal-themed treats—gummy sharks suspended in blue Jell-O, and decorated cookies cut into animal shapes through the use of large cookie cutters.

Hollie stood in front of the group in an apron with a paw-print pattern, a replica passed out to everyone else in attendance. "We talked today about how, when we're stressed, cooking can relax us. Especially when we tune into our five senses. Can anyone here name one of them?"

Little Pia's hand went up, the chunky sweater sleeve falling down to her elbows as she eagerly bounced. "Seeing?"

"Yes, sight," Hollie continued. "What are some colors we can see in these ingredients we're using today?"

Answers piled on top of each other from the little chefs.

"Blue Jell-O."

"Green gummy sharks."

"Yellow cookie dough and frosting that's purple, brown, orange, red…" An eager little boy took a deep breath as his mother put a hand on his shoulder to slow the flow of words.

Eliza clapped, impressed, chiming in to assist, "What about another sense?"

"Hearing?" another boy in a ballcap called out. "I bet the beaters make really loud noise. And when you squirt the frosting out, it sounds like—"

The rest of the sentence was swallowed up by childish giggles.

Next to Nolan, Gus inched forward in his seat, his pale blue eyes on Eliza. "I smell sugar and lemons. And the dough is cold. And we're gonna get to taste it soon."

Eliza held up her hand, counting off on her fingers. "Sight, touch, taste, smell and hearing. All five senses."

Grounding.

Using her senses.

At the moment, Eliza could use all the help she could get when it came to grounding herself. Anything to keep her heart from racing, anxiety cranking, over what would come next with Nolan. Anything to keep herself from counting off her own five senses, which activated keenly anytime he was around her. All rational thought insisted that him showing up here today was a coincidence. But she also couldn't help wondering how his last-minute event change had come right after she volunteered to help out here.

Could he have overheard? That seemed like a stretch.

Still, as she helped Hollie wrap up the session, she couldn't fight the urge to call on her senses. Too bad even those betrayed her, because right now, stroking her fingers along those sweater fibers wasn't distracting her one bit. Not with the sensory feast that Nolan provided.

Sight: the vibrant blue of Nolan's eyes. Sound: the husky timbre of his laugh. Scent: caramel, like the dessert on their date. And actually, caramel covered taste, too.

And touch? She wanted to ground herself in that sense with him most of all, her fingers remembering what it had felt like to steal over his strong shoulders and absorb the warmth of his body.

Now she just had to figure out what to do about it.

Nolan parked himself by the door leading out of Bone Appétit Café, not even slightly deterred by the chill that still seeped through the double-paned glass. No way was he letting Eliza slip past without having a conversation. All night long, he'd rehearsed what he planned to say to her, his pitch for how they should spend the rest of his last week at the ranch.

The children were enjoying their snacks, and if he stepped outside for a private discussion with Eliza, he could still see Gus and Mavis through the window being monitored by the café staff. Across the room, he watched Eliza pull off the paw-print apron and retrieve her parka and gloves.

"Hey, Eliza? Do you have a minute?" he asked. "I'd like to step outside so we can talk. I can keep an eye on the kids through the window."

"Um, okay." Her forehead creased in confusion as she shrugged on her winter jacket.

He swept open the door and motioned her through. As she stepped past him, she inhaled deeply, touching the icy lamp post, her eyes scanning the landscape dusted by flurries. Ice-skaters spun in circles on the distant outdoor rink. Squeals from the hill packed with people sledding and tubing carried on the wind. A bonfire puffed smoke into the air.

And he couldn't shrug aside the concern that she might be taking it all in, not just in a passing way, but grounding herself against a stressor, the way she and Hollie had just explained to the group.

Surely it was his imagination. Still... "Is something wrong? Did something happen? Are you feeling okay?"

A wry smile flickered across her face. "Nothing happened, Doctor. I'm feeling fine." She fidgeted with the zipper tab on her parka. "What did you need to talk about?"

He stuffed his hands into his jacket pockets to keep from reaching out for her, cupping her beautiful face highlighted by the afternoon sun. The last thing he wanted was to spook her before he even got to pitch his idea. "Ignoring each other isn't going so well for me. How about you?"

Her shoulders sagged, and she stopped looking all around. Instead, her attention became laser focused on him. She shifted in her boots, the movement crushing into the powdery snow beneath them. A small tug of a smile while her cheeks turned red from the rush of cold that barreled through the porch. "Me neither."

Those two simple words powered through him, affirming what he suspected but had barely dared let himself presume. She was just as drawn to him as he was to her.

Nolan reached, touching her elbow lightly as snow flurries kept streaming from the sky. "What do you propose we do about that?"

Frowning, she swept snowflakes off her face while other snowflakes decorated her caramel brown hair, making her look like some ethereal, fine-boned ice queen—with a steely spine. "I have no idea. But I'm open to suggestions."

Exactly what he'd been hoping to hear. "I suggest that we date."

Her eyes went wide in shock. An exhale billowed like smoke between them. "Date? The no-strings sort?"

"Sure, and the kids wouldn't be tagging along," he said, flipping the collar up on his coat as another gust of icy wind whipped through. "Mavis and Gus have times they're at play practice. They've also chosen a couple of events they want to do with their pals. Plus, there are their naps and bedtimes when a sitter can watch over them and I'm free to do other things. I have more flexibility here than I would have expected."

But then, the child-friendly nature of the operation had been highlighted in the ranch's literature. He just hadn't been able to envision how that would work when he'd first arrived. He couldn't have predicted how welcoming the place would be for children, let alone how safe. The kids were doing well.

"I'm listening," she said warily, crossing her arms over her body, hugging herself.

Defensively? Or just from the cold?

The urge to warm her himself was so strong he had to jam his hands deeper in his pockets to resist reaching out for her. He glanced back into the Bone Appétit Café briefly, making sure the kids were still right where he'd left them under the watchful eyes of Top Dog staffers. Gus and Mavis were still busily working on their animal-themed treats.

Allowing Nolan this moment to convince Eliza of his plan.

"I'm not pushing for a fling or making some kind of smarmy move on you," he reassured her. "I just want to spend time with you. If you want to spend that time in Moonlight Ridge, we can. But perhaps we could also look to the ranch for friendly activities. Enjoy each other's company while I'm here and agree that we'll say our good-byes when I leave for home next week."

Even if the thought of those goodbyes already formed a knot in his gut. Yet he couldn't imagine how to keep ignoring the attraction to her. It was a draw that wouldn't go away.

"That sounds…" Her face smoothed, her eyes

searching his for a long moment before she let out a slow breath. "Like an idea worth exploring."

Relief surged through him, more so than he would have expected or was comfortable analyzing at the moment. That could wait until later.

Right now, he wanted to make the most of the moment and celebrate the win of more time with her. "How about we take turns choosing the outings?"

A slow smile spread across her face, her whole aspect brightening. "All right. I'll send you my work schedule, you send me your kid-free times and we can go from there."

For the first time in longer than he could remember, Nolan was looking forward to tomorrow. He didn't want to overthink it, in spite of his naturally analytical nature.

Because he knew this decision to spend more time with Eliza was anything but logical.

Eliza knew going on dates with Nolan wasn't practical. But she was diving into the challenge with both feet all the same. Choosing their first outing had kept her awake until two in the morning, sitting in her bed under the skylight, cross referencing her schedule with times he had free from taking care of the kids.

Inspiration had struck with a mischievous slant. She'd decided to keep her idea a secret from him, and she couldn't wait to see his reaction when he realized what she had planned.

Together, they walked up the stone steps toward the main lodge, others leaving with to-go dinner boxes. Snow drifted down in fat, lazy flakes. Nolan's hand cupped her elbow carefully— a quaint gesture of protection that warmed her insides almost as much as the appreciation in his eyes when he'd come to her apartment to escort her over.

She'd hoped to strike the right balance between "making an effort" and "not going over the top." She'd chosen black skinny jeans with black leather boots, a flowing poet's shirt and a gray cashmere scarf. Her tweed coat made for a fun change from parkas and work jackets.

No question, she was enjoying this night already, thanks to Nolan.

Turning to him just outside the massive double doors, she took in the sight of him in jeans and a fur-lined, brown leather jacket that made her pulse leap in her veins. "Are you ready to learn our plans for the evening?"

"You've piqued my interest. Especially when you walked me the long way here."

The ease of their conversation during the stroll had made for the perfect end to a long workday. He'd even steadied her as they picked their way around icy patches. "Okay, then, here we go."

She swept the door wide and stepped into the lobby, the scents of a fragrant wood fire mingling with spicy, fruity notes from the mulled wine that was served on cold evenings. She gestured toward the living area. Leather sofas and chairs were full of guests participating in...

"A sewing circle?" Nolan asked, scratching his head under his knit cap. "You've signed us up for a knitting class?"

Eliza stifled a laugh. She'd been anticipating his reaction all day long. It had been worth the wait. She enjoyed the stunned expression on Nolan's face, followed by good-natured acceptance.

"Knitting *and* crocheting," Eliza clarified. "Are you still game for tonight's date?"

He peeled off his hat and gloves before shrugging out of his leather jacket. He collected her tweed coat and placed their winter gear on the antler coatrack to the left. "I'm all in. Just don't expect anything other than a tangled mess."

Eliza slid her arm through his and led him to a table covered with a wide array of different colors and textures of yarn, the flex of his muscles a delicious temptation. "I bet you'll be surprised." She pointed toward a grandmotherly type and said, "That's Celeste, the class leader. She owns a fabric store in Moonlight Ridge. Her granddaughter, Annie—" she nodded toward a college-aged student arranging skeins of yarn on a table "—helps out."

The duo had even dressed in matching jean jackets and pink boots. Eliza knew from guest evaluations that this team always led fun and informative sessions.

Nolan nodded, blowing into his cold hands for a moment. "Lead the way."

After choosing their materials—yellow alpaca wool for her and tan mohair for him—they snagged crochet needles and sat side by side on a leather love seat. His warm thigh pressed against hers, the scent of his spicy aftershave teasing her every breath. "I've been anxious to try all the activities Top Dog has to offer, but I'm so busy with work I don't always get the chance," she explained. "I appreciate you doing this with me."

This one had topped her list to check out for a long time since she wanted to connect with the needleworking memories she had of her mom.

Nolan pitched the yarn ball from one hand to the other as the others welcomed him. "I'm happy to be here. Trying new things is good for the brain."

A half dozen ladies of varying ages—including Jaqueline Tremaine—were seated around the fireplace, flames flickering. A little poodle was curled up asleep under Jacqueline's chair, the leash anchored by the chair leg.

Celeste clapped her hands together, her glasses on a rhinestone chain around her neck glinting from the overhead lights. "We'll be beginning in just a few minutes. We're waiting on one more guest to arrive. In the meantime, feel free to get a snack and chat. Or begin with a simple chain stitch explained in the handouts on the end tables."

Eliza looped the end of the yarn around her crochet needle, the wool silky against her skin. "Would you have signed up for this if I hadn't chosen it?"

He watched and mimicked the motion with his

own twine, ignoring the flyer. "Maybe I already know how."

"Seriously? You crochet?" Her hands fell to her lap. "Did you learn to make yourself better at stitching patients?"

"Nah, I was just pulling your leg." He elbowed her lightly. "I don't have a clue how to do this."

"That's why I chose to crochet rather than knitting. I think it's easier." She looped the needle through, starting her chain as her mother had showed her so many times, the activity soothing her for the connection it made her recall.

"I probably could have used a class like this when I was in med school. Maybe I'll sign us up for the quilting class."

She snorted on a laugh. Her mom had tried to teach her how to quilt, and it had been a disaster. Eliza tugged more yarn from her skein. "I'm working that day—and if I'm not, I will be."

"That's too bad." He chuckled softly, chained a few loops and then shot a look her way. "So, fill me in. What's the Top Dog purpose to this packtivity? Other than loosening up my fingers."

Eliza nodded toward the class leader, who had just paused near them to observe their work. "Maybe you can answer this better, Celeste?"

The older woman nodded. "It's calming. It can keep the mind sharp, especially the part of the brain that's used for mathematics." She stopped to glance back at Nolan. "Dr. Barnett, some studies show it lowers blood pressure."

Jacqueline displayed her white yarn, a half-lacy drape over her lap. "Then I'm going to crochet a king-sized blanket to get over what my husband did this morning." She reached down to pet her poodle, then scooped up the curly pup, who had bows on her ears. "I awoke today to find him playing video games. Why did we pay to come on this vacation if he's just going to stay on his headset while gaming with his friends back home?"

Another woman looked up from her project, which looked like a pastel rainbow baby blanket. "It's his vacation, too. Maybe that's what helps him to decompress, like watching ball games."

Eliza realized Nolan had gone still beside her. A quick glance over showed her that he was staring off in space, a frown etched on his face, his crocheted chain resting in his lap.

Tapping him on his graying temple, she whispered, "Hey, what's going on in there?"

His blue eyes cleared, meeting hers for a moment before sliding down to the yarn. "Just thinking about all the time I spent away from my family in med school, then building my part of the practice."

She understood well about regrets. She had spent years being torn between her desire to follow her own path and her parents' needs—and always feeling like she had come up short. But she also recognized that no words of reassurance from others could bring peace. At least, they hadn't for her.

So she opted for a different tactic. "From what I've seen, you're a good doctor. Tell me about some of your favorite cases—if you can."

His eyebrows shot up, and his fingers started moving along the yarn again, as if by rote. "Huh, well, let me think. I've never had someone ask me that before."

He paused, his fingers increasing speed on a chain so long it would likely need to be unraveled. But the activity itself was already serving another purpose: relaxing the room. Nolan included. So Eliza waited, soaking in the sight of his handsome face as he thought over her question.

"Well," he finally said, "I've pulled out my fair share of odd objects from kids' noses. It's funny to see what new things they'll wedge up there. Pebbles. LEGOs. Beans. Game pieces. The list goes on and on."

"Fascinating—" and the mental image of him with the children was charming "—but I thought you would have talked about diagnosing some exotic illness."

"Nah." He shook his head, a lopsided grin spreading over his face. "That's not nearly as interesting as a Polly Pocket up the nostril."

A laugh flew free, and she leaned against him, shoulder to shoulder. So close. So natural. Like they'd known each other far longer than just a week.

Before Eliza could unscramble her thoughts enough to answer him, Celeste announced that class was ready to begin now that the last attendee had arrived. The late arrival apologized and quickly sat cross legged on the floor in front of the fireplace, swinging her tapestry bag into her lap. Nolan was a good sport—all in, as he'd promised, laughing at himself as his yarn tangled.

Even as Eliza's hands worked by rote, her mind was still fully focused on the charming, modest man beside her. She'd expected to knock him off guard with this pack-tivity. Instead, she was the one whose world had been jostled seeing a more easygoing side to him. Open to new adventures. This date was already so much more than she'd expected.

And they hadn't yet arrived on her doorstep with the possibility of a kiss goodnight.

Chapter Ten

Nolan wondered if they would kiss. He wanted to—no doubt. And while he certainly was getting attraction vibes from her, he also wanted to be absolutely sure.

Luckily, he had the whole walk from the lodge to her place to figure it out. Side by side, they walked through the crisp night, snow drifting softly around them. Streetlights hung from wooden posts, lighting their path. Loki had been visiting with the O'Brien kids, and Eliza had retrieved the pup after leaving the crocheting/knitting class.

Now the border collie pranced in the snow, bounding from snowdrift to snowdrift, wearing himself out. Nolan wished the answer to his pent-up energy was as simple to achieve.

Moonbeams played with the honey-colored streaks in her brown hair. Her cheeks were pink from the cold, her smile so natural as she waved at a family of six racing by on their way to their cabin.

Eliza sidestepped her way past the firepit surrounded by tiki torches. "Thank you for being such a good sport tonight about the sewing circle."

"I actually enjoyed myself." Eliza's date choice had been a fun surprise—much like the woman. He pulled his finished crochet product from his pocket: a brown square. "If the doctor thing doesn't work out, I have a bright future making pot holders and washrags."

Her laughter mixed with his, twining in the puffs of white smoke billowing into the cold air. "You could give them out to patients instead of suckers and stickers."

"There would be a revolt in my young clientele," he said with a wink. "Now, if they could pet Loki here while getting vaccinations, that would go over much better. I'm certain he would be a big draw."

"See now, you're thinking about life the Top Dog way." A couple in their sixties stopped beneath a pine tree whose boughs were heavy with snow. The man pointed high into the treetop while the woman put her pink-gloved hand on her chest. Even in the muted light, Nolan noted what held their attention—a fluffy barn owl.

Eyes pulling back to Eliza, Nolan kept pace with her as they moved toward the barn. "Where did you get Loki? He's quite a character."

"Loki actually belongs to the ranch. He was dumped here at about six months old. We later figured out he came from a backyard breeder. Someone had taken him as a puppy, then returned him for being too active."

"Loki's a border collie. What did they expect?" As he stepped forward, a twig snapped beneath his boot, sending a cloud of snow upward onto his jeans. Cold leaked through the fabric.

"Exactly. Anyway, the backyard breeder figured since the O'Briens already had a border collie, they would have a soft spot for the breed. But when I started training Loki to herd sheep, he grew attached to me."

"He most definitely did." Nolan watched the way she guided the dog wordlessly with just hand gestures, sending him where she wanted, having him wait at a crosswalk to let another couple pass. She and the dog were so in tune that it was easy to miss their silent conversations.

"The O'Briens and I joke that we've got joint custody of Loki. Whoever is going to be home the most that day or even that evening, keeps him. He doesn't do well when he's left alone. He's a smart pup who needs an active lifestyle to keep his mind engaged in something other than mischief. It works best for him that way." For a moment, her gaze followed Loki as the dog snuffled under the snow near some bushes, tail wagging as his nose stirred at some dead leaves.

Nolan stepped over an icy patch, holding Eliza's elbow to steady her as the dog left his investigations to run ahead of them. "What a lucky thing for Loki you were able to train him."

"Lucky for me, too." As the icy trail narrowed, she walked closer to Nolan, the pathway lined with trees, twinkling lights on the branches. "Loki's always been sweet, but he needed to channel his prey drive and energy."

"Seeing him in action herding the sheep at the rodeo was pure magic. While you have a lovely voice and play the keyboard well, you were right that this is your calling."

Eliza laughed. "Even my mother had to concede that in the end. But she held on to that con-cert-pianist dream for a long time. She loved music, which is a part of why she pushed me so hard, I think." Shivering, she stuffed her hands into her pockets. "Mom was a music teacher at the middle school—she taught band and voice. My dad was a math teacher and the school's baseball coach. From the sixth grade on, I rode with one of them to and from school every day." Her teeth chattered on the last word.

Nolan draped an arm over her shoulders and tucked her to his side, taking heart as she bur-rowed closer. "You must miss them very much."

"I do. Every day." A shadow chased across her face, something different from grief.

"But?" he prompted.

"I feel guilty, sometimes, being this happy with my job and my life here at the ranch..." She paused, gesturing from the pasture to the snowcapped mountains. "Knowing that's only possible because they're gone."

He understood survivor's guilt all too well. A lump formed in his throat. "Moving forward is hard."

"Are your parents still alive?" She looked up at him, snowflakes in her long eyelashes.

"Yes, they are," he said, his mind still zeroed

in on the feel of Eliza close to him, the scent of her hair teasing his every breath. The perfect distraction from weighty thoughts. "Dad still clocks in at the office at seven every morning, sharp as a tack. Mom owns a flower shop that she runs full-time."

"Do Gus and Mavis get to spend much time with them? What a blessing for your parents to be able to know their great-grandchildren." She snapped her fingers for Loki to move closer to her side, away from another couple walking their dog.

The path forked, one trail leading to cabins, the other toward the main stable and her second-floor apartment. A light whinny of horses from inside the barn drifted on the wind.

"They offer, but kids that young are difficult to keep up with." And he could understand that. Parenting Gus and Mavis was the toughest thing he'd ever done. Ever. "They are of the mindset I should get a live-in nanny."

"And you're against that?" she asked, her voice so neutral he couldn't get a read off her stance.

"I was brought up by a nanny," he answered simply. "I want to be the one who reads the kids their bedtime stories." He'd missed out on the time with his son. He wasn't going to repeat the mistake.

She looked up at him. "Is that why you've been so resistant to using the ranch's sitter service?"

He gave a noncommittal grunt, tipping his head to the sky.

Stopping, she pivoted to face him at the base of the outdoor stairs leading up to her apartment. "I'm sorry. I didn't mean to presume…"

Her words were cut short by Loki circling them, the leash tangling around their legs.

"Don't give it another thought." Nolan braced his hands on her arms to keep her from falling, standing chest to chest, so close, an almost embrace. "I think Loki is matchmaking."

A grin lighting her eyes, she glanced down at her dog, then back at him. "Nudging us to a doorstep kiss at the end of the date?"

"I didn't mean to presume," he repeated her words, his voice lowering.

"You're not," she answered, leaning closer.

That was all the invitation he needed.

He lowered his mouth to hers, kissing her with the snow drifting down around them. The moment was heavy with the kind of romance he would have thought he was too old, too jaded, to appreciate. He was wrong. In fact, right now, he felt like a teenager again, finishing up a date with the new girl in town. And he was crazy into her.

Would it be so wrong to sink into those feelings—pretend he was young again and carefree, with nothing weighing him down or holding him back? No thoughts of what could happen down the road? Just keep enjoying these encounters during the remainder of his time at the Top Dog Dude Ranch?

As he eased back from their kiss, his heart hammering against his rib cage, Nolan knew that regardless of the consequences, he was already anticipating their next evening out.

The next day, after Eliza had finished leading the morning trail rides, she raced to the main lodge in search of Hollie. Eliza's parka flapped around her as she jogged carefully around patches of ice on her way to the private entrance to the O'Briens' quarters. She'd already texted Hollie that she was on her way and had permission to come straight back to the lodge's industrial kitchen.

She angled through the back entrance, down the corridor lined with photos of the family and pets. Breathlessly, she rushed into the kitchen and collapsed back against the log wall. The kitchen spread out in front of her with dark wooden cabinets and top-of-the-line stainless appliances.

Hollie, with paw-print oven mitts on her hands, was pulling a pound cake pan from the oven. Her matching Top Dog paw-patterned apron was cinched around her waist, her dark hair pulled back in a long braid. An island filled the middle space, surrounded by tree-stump bar-stools, with Charlotte Pace chopping fresh herbs, containers lined up in front of her.

The scent of cloves, home and friendship washed over Eliza, reminding her why she was here. "Ladies, I need help."

Charlotte pivoted on the bar stool, her blond hair gathered in a top knot. Her snow boots were beside the seat, her feet covered in thick orange socks. "What's wrong?"

Hollie set the cake pan on a cooling rack and tossed the pot holders into a basket. Concern creased her face, furrowing her brow. "Let me know whatever I can do. Just name it."

Drawing in a bracing breath, Eliza exhaled hard and admitted, "I need a party dress."

Just saying the words made her face heat.

Smiling, Hollie motioned for her to sit on one of the tree-stump stools. "Like a ball gown?"

"Not quite that extreme." Eliza took her place beside Charlotte, while Hollie stayed across from them. "Something flirty, like a little black dress—but one where I won't freeze to death in this weather. I've learned that my wardrobe is pretty limited when it comes to anything other than stable gear. I need something to borrow, if you don't mind."

Nolan hadn't given her any details on their date tonight, other than to dress for a party and wear her dancing shoes.

Hollie leaned closer on her elbows, her eyes full of curiosity. "Where are you going?"

"On a date." Her stomach fluttered, still amazed she could feel this way so quickly about someone. But her time with Nolan left her feeling hyperaware, all her senses highly attuned. After their last date, she'd replayed the kiss over and over in her mind. "With Nolan Barnett."

Both women squealed, scooting their barstools even closer to the island.

Charlotte extended her hand across the island toward Hollie. "Pay up."

Hollie reached into a bone-shaped cookie jar beside her and pulled out a twenty. "You were right. Their crocheting class wasn't a one-off, accidental meeting."

Eliza hated being so transparent—another sign that she was behaving every bit as much like a teenager, as she'd feared. She thought she'd been careful to keep things low-key. "Was I that obvious?"

"Girlfriend…" Charlotte fanned her hand in front of her face. "The chemistry between you two is off the chain. We both noticed. The bet was on whether you two were acting on it. I voted yes and Hollie voted no."

Searching Hollie's face, Eliza asked, "That's not a problem, right? Given that I work here and he's a guest?"

Hollie waved aside the concern. "Not at all. As long as you're doing your job, we're happy. Your personal time is your business and so is who you choose to spend it with. Now, as your friend, I want details because no one's buying that you two just happened to both attend a crocheting class together."

Fair point. She might as well have taken out an ad broadcasting their new arrangement. "We both tried ignoring the attraction since he's leaving in a week and lives far away. But that wasn't working so well for us. We agreed to go out on dates—no strings, no pressure. Just fun outings. We take turns choosing the venue."

Charlotte pushed aside the cutting board full of herbs and angled closer. "How many of these *no-string dates* have you been on?"

"Two," she admitted, the memory of both outings—and both kisses—tingling through her. "We went to Moonlight Ridge for a late dinner and a ride on the ski lift."

Charlotte pressed a hand to her chest. "Romantic. Declan should be taking notes."

Hollie tapped Eliza on the hand. "Maybe Dr. Barnett could lead a master class in dating for our attendees. I'll make sure Jacob attends, too. Meanwhile, I have to know—how did the crocheting class go? I was dying to ask when you picked up Loki."

"Really well, actually. He seemed to enjoy it and made a fairly good pot holder. Or maybe it was a washrag. I'm not sure," she said with laughter that faded as she thought back through her strange choice. "I think in some way I was testing him to see if he meant it when he said he wasn't going to put any pressure on me for a hookup. Because no matter how attracted we are to each other, neither of us needs any kind of complication in our lives right now."

"Fair enough," Hollie said, shaking her head in a way that said she wasn't buying the explanation for a second. "Now, let's scour my closet for a sexy dress for you to wear to the next date."

Sexy?

Eliza definitely hadn't included that in her list of outfit requirements. But who was she to argue when her thoughts were all circling in that direction with Nolan? Gathering her courage, she followed Hollie out of the kitchen, already imagining Nolan's reaction to a sexy dress.

Thank goodness the ranch was wearing out the kids so that bedtime was a piece of cake.

Now that Nolan had Gus and Mavis settled into their beds, and a ranch sitter in the cabin's living room, he was free to pick up his date. Taking the steps up to Eliza's apartment two at a time, he gripped the railing even though the planked stairs had been heavily salted.

Nolan had thought through a number of ideas for their next date—considered each one, then discarded it. It was tough to follow up her whimsical choice. Finally, he decided to go in the total opposite direction.

So much of their time together had been spent reflecting, which of course was the overall mission of the ranch. But the place was also about fun. Something two workaholics like Eliza and him didn't indulge in all that often. And close by so they didn't spend half the evening in the car, driving to and fro.

As he reached the landing, she opened her door.

The sight of her knocked the breath from his body. She'd always been lovely. Tonight, though? She was smoking hot.

She wore a body-hugging sweater dress with silver piping and black leather high-heeled boots. Her pewter chandelier earrings played peekaboo in her loose hair as she turned her head. A black wool coat was draped over her arm.

"Hello," she said, her lips slick with a pale pink gloss.

"You look…incredible." He reached out to help her put on her coat, allowing himself a moment to skim his hands along her shoulders.

She looked back at him. "You too— handsome, I mean."

Their eyes held for a charged moment, and he dropped a quick kiss on her mouth. So simple. So right. Easy to make a habit. Too easy.

Stepping back, he offered his arm. "We're not going much further. Just to the far barn." The ranch had stables and the arena, but there were also two more barns, one of which was being used for a birthday party.

"The Ekholm party? Celebrating Mr. Ekholm's sixty-fifth birthday?" The family had really gone all out for him, even hiring his favorite jazz singer to perform. Her eyebrows pinched together as she cleared the last step. "It sounds amazing, but I'm confused how we got an invitation. I'm not comfortable being a party-crasher, especially as an employee. It might reflect badly on the O'Briens."

He could understand her concern. The last thing he wanted was for her to feel uncomfortable.

"No worries on that account," he assured her, steering her toward the barn already vibrating with music. "I chatted with them over breakfast the first week and answered a medical question for them, giving them the name of a specialist. They invited me to the party then, and I didn't think anything of it… Then it hit me that it could be a fun date with dancing."

"Okay, then. Count me in." Eliza walked beside him toward the barn already glowing with a bower of twinkling lights over the wide double doors. "What did the kids do today? I missed seeing them."

The genuine note in her voice tugged at him.

And yeah, it felt nice to have someone to tell about the cute things they'd done. To share notes with at the end of the day. It made life feel less... lonely.

"Gus chose an activity with his new friends Benji, Elliot and Phillip. Something about junior spelunking in the Sulis Springs cave. Mavis and I went to art class. It's amazing how many shapes we can make from tracing a hand."

He flexed his fingers in his gloves, recalling the slew of animals they'd created from Mavis's tiny hands—a peacock, an octopus, a chicken, a spotted cow... The front of his refrigerator would be full when they got home. Fast on the heels of that thought, he wondered how he would find time to make more memories like this when he returned back to work.

And then he lost track of his thoughts altogether at the simple brush of her coat against his leg.

Eliza stuffed her hands into her coat pockets as they reached the barn, her heels crunching snow. He swung open the barn door, eyes adjusting to the warm glow of the chandelier hanging from the exposed pine beams of the barn's ceiling. Soft white tulle cascaded elegantly down the walls.

Couples laughed, wineglasses clinking at the tables with pale yellow linens. Fairy lights trailed from the ceiling to create a photo booth backdrop.

Notes of a heartfelt saxophone solo caught his attention, sending his foot tapping. Nolan's head swiveled toward the small stage, where the band played old jazzy pop. He felt right at home in this environment, which was so like dozens of events he'd attended for professional schmoozing.

And yet it was all new—special—with Eliza by his side.

He helped her off with her coat, resisting the urge to linger as the scent of her shampoo wafted past his nose. Instead, he passed her jacket over to the young coat check attendant.

Eliza smiled over her shoulder at him. "Nolan, you're going to be tired burning the midnight oil. I'd always heard parents should nap when the children sleep."

The mischievous look in her eyes stirred him, making him hungry to find a reason to have her in his arms as soon as possible.

"I've suddenly lost my interest in napping." At the moment, he was very, very wide awake and on fire from wanting her. "You've lightened my mood lately."

"It's the ranch. This place is the best," she said, her voice full of pride as they walked deeper into the party.

The way she demurred, pushing all praise onto the ranch, reminded him of how driven she was in her profession and how committed she was to this place. Something he understood all too well, given his own workaholic devotion to his family's practice. Sure, it gave them a lot in common. But that strong commitment leading them in different directions would also pull them apart at the end of this week.

A thought that shouldn't trouble him as much as it already did.

"Whatever you say. The last thing I want to do this evening is argue." He stepped closer to her, easing out of the way of a waiter carrying a tray of drinks.

Eliza extended her arms just as the band shifted to a slow dance, an old-school Sinatra tune. "Then let's dance."

What a lovely picture she made, her hair glinting in the twinkle lights, her full lips curving in a smile that was just for him. Desire shot through him.

He shoved aside concerns and doubts, pinning his focus on this moment, this woman. Sweeping her into his arms, he steered them toward the dance floor, feet moving in perfect sync, bringing to light the fatal flaw in his plan.

Having her in his arms all evening long was going to be sweet torture.

Chapter Eleven

Charlotte sank deeper into the churning waters of the Sulis Springs Cave, the scent of sulfur tinging the air. Her body soaked in the warmth, leaving her languid.

Or maybe that was from the sexy sheriff occupying the waters with her. Just the two of them. Alone. No demands from the outside world.

There were many perks of working at the Top Dog Dude Ranch—like living in a quaint cabin and eating at the amazing dining hall. But staff also received vouchers to use on some of the luxury facilities when they weren't reserved by other guests.

She'd helped set up for a bridal shower in the ranch's Sulis Springs Cave earlier in the day, which was when she had realized there was an open slot in the schedule tonight—a rarity. So she'd slotted a couple of hours for herself. The bubbling hot springs inside offered healing on both a physical and spiritual level. And right now, Charlotte needed everything the famed springs had to offer.

Cave walls were periodically painted by guests in art therapy classes, the images depicting their history, joys and pains. Pottery also lined the walls, pieces created by visitors of all ages. Candles were lined up around the water's edge, and classical music echoed softly from her cell phone as she tried to let go of everything but this moment. It wasn't an easy task.

She was struggling to balance work, her new relationship with Declan and keeping Rory from setting his world on fire. She understood her brother was hurt by a long history of bad memories with their mother and father. Her parents' defection had hit him in different ways that she couldn't have predicted, but she was doing her best to be supportive. And while she carried those heartaches from their broken family as well, she was an adult. She just hoped she was adult enough to do right by her sibling at this crucial time in his young life.

Thank goodness Declan had been so flexible about working around her crazy schedule. Her heart leapt as she took in the sight of him swimming closer, his muscled arms slicing through the water. Steam rose around him. She could hardly believe she'd pulled this off—an evening's romantic getaway with Declan.

Tonight, they'd taken their relationship to the next level. Her body still tingled in the aftermath of making love in the cave—such a beautifully romantic setting.

Extending a hand to him, she tugged him to sit beside her on the rock ledge seat in the springs. "You're too far away," she teased. "I miss you."

He grasped her by the waist and pulled her to straddle his lap. "Hello, gorgeous. I've missed you, too. It's been at least three minutes since I touched you."

His gravelly voice rumbled his chest against hers.

She stroked back a damp lock from his forehead. "Thank you for meeting me here."

"Thank you for being you." He angled a kiss over her mouth, his broad palms against her waist. "I hope you know how incredible you are.

This evening with you… It was…" He paused, whistling low.

She couldn't agree more. Their chemistry when making love had blindsided her. Already her body hummed for more. But there was no rush. She wanted the evening to last. He'd brought a picnic. She'd supplied a thick quilt.

"I'm sorry we have to sneak around so much for time alone. I'm just not comfortable having you sleep over because of Rory. I know we're adults, and we don't owe anyone an explanation, but…" She wanted to avoid anything that caused more controversy with her brother. The fights between them were already difficult enough.

"Say no more. He's a teenager." His smile faded and he shifted her from his lap to her seat beside him again. "Trust me, I understand."

His arm slid around her shoulders, and she nestled against him. "It's a scary responsibility, looking out for him," she admitted.

"Rory doesn't make it easy," he said wryly.

No kidding. "I appreciate your help with him. You set such a powerful example of a successful, strong man."

Stroking her face, fingers tunneling into her hair, he said, "Flattery will get you everywhere."

"That's my hope." She wriggled against him.

Chuckling, he slipped his arms around her and stood, water sheeting from their bodies as he walked up the stone steps toward their quilt and dinner. Towels were folded by the picnic basket—the perfect date waiting to be enjoyed with the perfect man. When they arrived at the waiting blanket, he set her down. Their fingers linked, she playfully drew him down with her.

From a few feet away, resting on her discarded clothes, her phone chimed with an incoming text. A reminder of real life and all the problems she'd wanted to leave behind when she entered the cave tonight. The tug-of-war going on inside of her strengthened—her job, her brother, her growing feelings for this man were all pulling at her, and she didn't have a clue how to keep the constant pressure from tearing her apart. She battled to keep the anxiety in check, to enjoy the evening and the peace that had come before this moment.

Declan reached for a towel. "You should check that. Maybe it's your brother."

The anxiety worsened as she swallowed the fear of any new problems concerning Rory.

"Or maybe it's work. But hopefully it's spam." Sighing in frustration, she flattened a palm to Declan's chest and reached for her cell with her other. "Hold that thought."

Wrapping a towel around her body, she grabbed the phone, finding what she feared most—what Declan seemed to have already guessed. The message was from her brother, a second and third text following fast on its heels.

The first message read, I know I wasn't supposed to go out tonight, but I did.

She scrolled to the second: And I'm locked out of the house.

Which brought her to what would no doubt end her time away: I need you to come home and let me inside before I freeze to death.

The wad of tension in her gut tightened painfully.

Sighing, she set her phone down and reached for her clothes, knowing there was no other option but to help her sibling. "It's Rory. I'm sorry, but I have to go."

Her pocket of peace with Declan was over, and she had no idea when—or how—they would find another.

Eliza never would have guessed going to a stranger's party would be so fun. But Nolan had made it an evening to remember.

Her head still spinning from dancing, her body deliciously tired, she held his hand on the short walk back toward the stables. Their fingers linked in a way that made her think about how well they fit together on multiple levels. They'd spent most of the time in each other's arms, tearing up the dance floor, their steps perfectly in sync. While she hadn't chased her mother's dream of becoming a concert pianist, she'd never lost her ear for music, and the five-star band had been a treat to listen to all night.

And the prime-rib dinner? She nearly groaned in bliss at the memory. "You sure know how to pick the right shindig."

The glow of the evening still clung to her, making her feel connected to him in ways beyond their linked hands. She fought the urge to tip her forehead to his shoulder so she could savor more of his warmth, his strength.

"Glad you enjoyed yourself. The ranch is, quite possibly, one of the most incredible vacation spots I've ever visited. And it struck me that sometimes, it must get old for you, standing on the sidelines with other ranch employees while everyone else indulges in the fruits of your labors."

"You're right. It was fun getting to enjoy the event without being tired from the setup." She sidestepped two teens walking a pair of dogs—

a shepherd mix and a confident poodle taking the lead.

She'd never considered herself the partying type. Growing up, she'd spent her nights and weekends perfecting her schoolwork and practicing her piano so her parents would okay her part-time job working with horses. While she'd loved college, keeping her GPA high enough to maintain her scholarship was crucial. Her parents had been approaching retirement, and she hadn't wanted to be a financial drain on them. Then afterward…

They'd needed her. Any free time had been spent on the riding school's horses, a benefit of working at the stables. Her hand was always first to go up when the boarders needed exercising. It centered her whenever she was troubled or drained from caregiving, bringing her peace.

Nolan squeezed her hand lightly. There was a deer at the edge of the field behind him, just visible in the moonlight. "Are you going to tell me all the therapeutic aspects of dancing?"

"I'm off the clock." Casting a sideways glance at her handsome escort, she added, "Remember? I'm here to party tonight."

"Okay, then, as a doctor, I'll tell you." He clapped a gloved palm to his chest, just over the lapel of his coat. "It improves heart function and lifts your mood."

"So it's good for the body *and* the mind."

His blue eyes locked in on her, bright and intense in the moon's hazy glow. "You're good for me."

Her heart stuttered in her chest. "Nothing serious tonight," she said to remind herself as much as to remind him. "Remember?"

"I hope you won't take this the wrong way, but how has no man scooped you up? You're an incredible woman."

"Maybe I haven't wanted to be scooped up by anyone I've met so far." She shot him a side-long look. "I'm a workaholic, for starters. But in answer to your question, I was close to get-ting married a couple of years ago, but it didn't work out."

"I'm sorry. Do you mind if I ask what hap-pened?" Nolan's voice dipped an octave, soft and tender, as their pace slowed.

She stared off into space for a moment, pro-cessing his question, wondering how much she wanted to share. A few yards ahead, she caught sight of a Moonlight Ridge Police Department vehicle pulling up outside of Charlotte's cabin. She frowned, worried, until she saw her friend step out of the passenger side and race up the path to her porch—where Rory was sitting in a rocker.

Drawing her attention back to Nolan, Eliza said, "We had a difference of opinion about my parents' care. He wanted me to move three states away. I wasn't comfortable leaving them." She shrugged. No need to share the ugly details of their final fight. She simply couldn't believe it had taken her five years to realize he'd only been waiting around in hopes her parents would pass away so the subject of moving wouldn't be an issue.

She was better off without him.

And what unsettled her all the more? Nolan's draw was already stronger than anything she'd felt before— even with her boyfriend of several years. She wasn't sure of a lot, but one thing she knew for certain.

She wasn't ready to say goodnight. Fluffing her hair to the side, Eliza opted to indulge. Her desire to spend time with this man was palpable with every heartbeat, every inhale of cold night laced with hearth-fire smoke from nearby cabins.

Stopping at the base of the stairs leading to her apartment over the stables, she rested a hand on his forearm. "I need to check on the kittens in my office real quick. If you're not in a hurry, would you like to come up for a cup of coffee by the fire?"

Nolan stood at Cricket's stall, waiting for Eliza while she checked on the kittens. His mind churned with surprise over her offer to go up to her place for coffee. He didn't want to assume the offer was anything more than an extension of their talking. She'd been clear about keeping things between them uncomplicated. And if he was honest with himself, he was enjoying their dates more than he could have imagined.

So yeah, he looked forward to spending time with her upstairs, even if all they did was drink coffee and learn more about each other.

Cricket stuck her head out of her stall, neck extended as she nudged Nolan. Scratching the horse on the neck, Nolan took in the quiet scene. Cricket nickered in what appeared to be delight, her bright red blanket contrasting against her brown fur. Nearby, other horses were also outfitted in blankets to guard against the cold as they munched on the fresh hay in their stalls. Moonbeam walked in a circle, filled with a surprising amount of energy for the evening.

He stroked the horse's velvety neck. "Cricket, girl, Eliza surprised me with that invitation for coffee. Not that I'm assuming anything, mind you. I'm just glad she wants this evening to last longer."

But he was hoping for more. He'd even prepared, bringing condoms. Not assuming. Just… wanting.

His hand trailed away from Cricket as he gravitated toward the open door leading to Eliza's office. A pale strip of light shone out over the dirt floor. Soft mewling sounds from the kittens drifted into the night, along with a hint of the low music she kept on in her office for them.

The sight of her kneeling beside the crate of kitties had him bracing a hand against the doorframe, the rest of the office fading as his focus narrowed to just her. Her coat was open and pooling on the floor around her. The fringe on her scarf dangled forward, enticing one of the little gray tabbies to bat playfully.

Eliza's laugh dusted the air with music. "Hello, little ones. Did you have fun today with all the people? I heard they enjoyed playing with you. Maybe you'll find new homes with somebody you met today?"

The soft lilt to her voice, the gentle float of her hands as she tended to the tiny striped furballs, lulled them into peaceful play in much the same way he'd seen her soothe the horses. Dogs. Sheep. All the animals here, actually. They knew her and trusted her.

Would he ever stop being mesmerized by these glimpses of all the many facets to her? She was, quite simply, breathtaking from every angle.

"Eliza," he said, just to test the feel of her name on his tongue.

Jolting, she looked back over her shoulder. "Oh my goodness." She cradled a kitten in each hand and carefully placed them back on the pet bed in the kennel. "You startled me. I thought you were staying out there with Cricket."

"Do you mind? Or should I go?" He gestured back toward the stalls. "I thought I would say hello to the kittens."

No sense confessing he couldn't stay away from her.

"Well, actually..." Blushing, she stood, swiping her hands down her sweater dress to brush away the cat fur. "You seeing my office might spoil the surprise of my next date choice for you."

"Oh really? I'm intrigued." He looked around at the leather sofa, the wooden desk, searching for a clue.

"I don't normally keep all of this in my office." She pointed toward the rope hammock in the shadowy corner, attached to two hooks in the log walls. A puffy cream-colored fleece blanket was folded neatly by a pillow. Then she gestured to the candles on top of the bookshelf.

"A hammock and candles." He tried to piece together what this next date might include.

"I know you said you're okay with all the late nights and early mornings at the ranch so we can spend time together, but I thought you might enjoy…."

His gaze went back to the hammock, and he teased dryly, "Don't tell me you think Grandpa needs a nap."

She pressed a hand to her lips, eyes wide. "No, that's not what I meant at all. You said napping is your 'hobby.' And everything you've told me about yourself shows how you push and push yourself—for work and for your family. I compiled some info I've learned here and put together for you a Top Dog Dude Ranch recipe for the perfect rest. I'll see you after, when you're refreshed."

"I'm intrigued," he said. And he was. He enjoyed seeing how this woman's mind worked. She was always full of surprises.

And it wasn't crocheting this go-round.

Curious about this so-called next date, he asked, "What about the kids?"

"I've got it covered," she reassured him. "Tomorrow, while you're here in the hammock, they'll be practicing the songs for the little production with the band. Afterward, children are invited to have lunch and nap time. Once they wake up, I'll bring carryout supper if you wish— with your permission, of course."

"Gus and Mavis will enjoy that as much as I will." He enjoyed hearing how much she'd thought through the day, right down to how he could manage the kids and still have time for a date.

"I got the idea for this perfect nap date from one of the pack-tivities we offer about ways to enhance a person's quality of sleep. Things like lavender scent, darkened space. A snack like bananas and almond butter. Your choice of chamomile tea or valerian root—"

"Valerian root tea? Does it taste as gross as it sounds?" He stepped deeper into the office and leaned a hip against her desk, nudging aside a block of wood with words burned into the grain: *The horse is God's gift to mankind.* —Arabian proverb.

"With honey, of course." Her smile turned playful.

"You've thought of everything." Unable to resist her allure any longer, he extended his arms, waiting.

Hoping.

She clasped his fingers, and he pulled her close, keeping his seat leaning against the edge of her desk.

"Everything?" She stepped between his legs, standing face-to-face with him. "I hope so."

Their kiss was natural, fluid, her mouth against his, and he slid his arms around her, anchoring her to him. Anchoring himself in the sensation of her.

She gripped his shoulders, her fingers digging in as she breathed against his lips. "Did you still want to come upstairs? And to be clear, I'm not just talking about a cup of java."

A huge sigh of relief rolled out of him because yes, that's what he wanted. More than air. "I was hoping that's what you meant." Still, he had to ask. "And you're sure?"

She toyed with his hairline along his neck.

"I think we can both agree that ignoring the attraction didn't work. And dating has only made the chemistry stronger. So the next logical step would be…"

Chuckling, he stood, keeping his arms around her, his gaze locked on her carefree face. "Do you really think this is about logic?"

"Actually, *logic* is probably a poor choice of words," she said, swaying closer, her breasts pressing against the wall of his chest. "That sounded much better in my mind."

Since they had the whole evening ahead of them, he allowed himself to steal another kiss— the slow and thorough kind that stirred promises of more.

There were so many reasons this would be a bad idea. She'd been upfront from the start that she was focused fully on launching her career— and he admired that about her. After all she had sacrificed for her family, this was—and should be—her turn.

He also understood that he didn't have the room in his life to devote to a relationship. And perhaps that's what made this moment possible for both of them. Neither of them had the mistaken notion that there was a feasible future between them. A thought that stung him more than it should. She was the most fascinating woman he'd met in longer than he could remember.

And if tonight was all he could have, then he was taking whatever she would offer.

Chapter Twelve

Sinking into the heat of Nolan's kiss, Eliza didn't doubt her decision to sleep with him for even a second. She wanted this night with Nolan. She needed to understand the irresistible draw between them. And this evening might well be her only chance to make the memory. She'd suffered enough regrets in her life for things beyond her control.

Tonight wouldn't be about regrets. And it was very much in her power to make it happen. So choosing to be with Nolan? Every fiber of her shouted a resounding yes.

They stood in her office, his arms around her, hers around him. She pressed against him, taking her time with the kiss, enjoying the fact that at this point, finally, she didn't have to deal with doubts insisting she pull away.

She thought about inviting him up to her apartment. But that seemed so very far away when she was on fire for him right now. And given the way he was holding her, kissing her, she could tell he was burning for her in return.

His mouth grazing from her lips to her ear, he whispered, "Just so you know, I've brought protection. But are you certain this is what you want?"

"Yes. Yes. Yes, again," she said, punctuating each *yes* with a kiss. She appreciated that he was being careful with her. In her chest, her heart rattled wildly as she took a steadying breath, the scent of evergreen grounding her. "You said no-strings dating. And I agreed."

He angled back, his blue eyes serious as he gazed down at her. "We agreed no-strings *dating*—not sex."

"Oh, Nolan." She sighed, her fingers grazing the flecks of silver dusting his temples. "I believe we've both known this was inevitable."

"I hoped so." A hefty exhale shuddered though

him that spoke of relief more than any words. "Didn't dare imagine it, though. The timing is…"

"Perfect," she reassured him. She searched his face, finding only desire. As he moved closer to her, the dim light cast his shadows along her office walls, a subtle movement that caught her attention. In fact… "Right now. In my office."

"Really? You'll get no argument from me," he said with a husky growl before a teasing light glimmered in his eyes. "Although, I hope you don't expect us to make this happen in the hammock. Because I don't consider myself ancient, but we might break something."

Giggles bubbled inside. She adored the unexpected playfulness he'd just brought to the moment. "Agreed. I was thinking of the sofa, because it feels like such a long way upstairs."

"You are a brilliant, beautiful woman." He backed away to close the door between her office and the stables. A click of the lock sent her senses into high alert, anticipation running through her limbs.

She lit the scented candles, a trace of vanilla and lavender already drifting toward her while he switched the music to a classical station. Snagging the soft fleece off the hammock, she unfurled it open onto the sofa.

Perfection.

She never would have imagined all those months ago when she first saw him at the physical therapist's office in Chattanooga that he would land here, at the ranch—with her.

Soon to be in her arms again.

Returning to him, she stood in front of Nolan for three heartbeats, just looking into his flame-bright blue eyes. Then, with slow, deliberate hands, she swept his winter coat from his broad shoulders, caressed down his strong arms and draped the jacket across her desk.

His pupils dilated with desire as he untwined her scarf slowly, kissing every inch of her neck until finally, the cashmere length slithered free. She shivered, awareness tingling through her as her head fell back. She thought he tossed the scarf onto the hammock, but she was too distracted by his mouth landing on hers again to be sure. Lids falling closed, she gave herself up to the sensations he stirred, his tongue stroking along hers, heightening her senses, making her want more. Her fingers hooked into the placket of his shirt, hungry for the feel of his skin against hers. With restless hands, they undressed each other.

Her, tugging his shirt from his pants and making fast work of the buttons.

Him, peeling her sweater dress over her head.

Back and forth, taking turns until they stood naked together, their clothing a tangled mass of cotton and lace on the hammock. His eyes stroked her with unmistakable appreciation that fanned the flames higher inside her. After one look at his muscular body, she couldn't wait another second to be in his arms, his bold hands roving, caressing. And she was all too eager to reciprocate—touching, learning and appreciating the landscape of him.

One deliberate step at a time, he walked her backward toward the sofa until her calves bumped the edge of the cushions. Her legs folded as he lowered her to the couch, leather creaking even as the fleece blanket teased along her oversensitive skin.

Even as she tried to urge him to go faster, he insisted on taking his time, drawing the sweet thread of desire tauter until finally—thank goodness—they were one. His body moving over hers. Her pulse speeding, her flesh tingling, awash in sensation.

How easily they learned one another's bodies, how in tune they were with one another, so that when the finish came for them both, it was as perfect as every other way they'd been in sync.

Afterward, she lay in his arms, trying to convince herself that the power of her feelings was simply due to the fact it had been so long since she'd been with a man. Nolan was the first since her fiancé two years ago. As quickly as the thought came to mind, it iced her insides, all but chilling the perspiration on her skin. Thinking of her two years of abstinence said too much about the importance of this moment, reminding her of the undeniable truth that she'd never been the sort to indulge in flings.

Which left her with absolutely no idea where she and Nolan stood now.

Two hours later, Nolan tucked Eliza against his side, gazing up through the skylight over her bed and wishing the moon would stop moving. He knew he would have to leave soon and relieve the sitter.

But for now, he could linger awhile longer.

He could enjoy the feel of her soft skin and gentle curves against him. Savor the memories of making love to her in her office and again in her apartment. Draw in the scent of her freshly washed hair and the memories it stirred of them showering together.

For now, he didn't want to think of anything but Eliza in his arms.

Shifting under the quilt to wriggle closer, she teased her fingers along his chest. "You're going to need that hammock tomorrow. I bet Mavis and Gus wake up early."

"Is that a hint for me to clear out?" He clasped her hand and held it over his heart. He couldn't help but smile as she adjusted the quilt while nestling closer. Floral notes of her soap and shampoo flooded his senses.

"Not at all." She angled up to look into his eyes, the quilt anchored to her chest. "I'm only showing concern for you."

"What about you?" He lifted a lock of her hair, testing it between his fingers before tucking it behind her ear. "I imagine your day starts early here on the ranch."

"It does. But I have only myself to look after at the end of the day." Shadows chased through her eyes before she rested her head on his shoulder again, shielding her face from him. "I loved my parents and don't regret one day I spent helping them. But being their caregiver for nearly two decades…" Her voice trailed off.

He tightened his arm around her, wishing he'd been there to comfort her then as she'd shouldered the weight of their care. "I hear what you're saying. I've seen it with the families of many patients with particularly challenging diagnoses."

Loki, who had been sound asleep for some time, let out a high-pitched yawn. Stretching, he readjusted, his moose dog toy falling from the fluffy dog bed in the corner of the room to the wood floor.

She rested her head back on Nolan's shoulder, draping her slim leg over his, her foot stroking his calf. "I can only imagine."

His memory filled with so many patients over the years, but in particular with a four-year-old little girl—Selena—whom he'd diagnosed with leukemia. While she'd been referred to an oncologist, he'd still been the family pediatrician for her and her siblings. He'd seen the toll of the thirty-seven-month battle—yes, thirty-seven; he remembered to the day when Selena had died. At the request of the family, he'd been with them all in the hospital room. Afterward, the weight of grief, of defeat, had been etched in every face.

Bringing his thoughts back to the present, he realized that up to now, he'd shared far more of his past with Eliza than she had about her life.

He tipped her chin up until he could see her and she could see his full attention. "What were their conditions? If you don't mind my asking."

Eliza paused, staring into his eyes for a long moment. The familiar lines of grief tightened the corners of her mouth. She exhaled before looking away, eyes drifting to Loki. The black-and-white border collie had drifted back to sleep, but his paws twitched as if he was dreaming.

Another exhale and she turned back to face him.

"Mom had early-onset Alzheimer's. Dad had heart and vascular troubles, strokes slowly chipping away at his health. They were older when they had me. Like any child, I didn't fully grasp I would lose my parents earlier than my contemporaries."

He kissed the top of her head. Moonbeams from the skylight over the bed washed over her, blanketing Eliza in an ethereal glow. "I didn't mean to bring up painful matters. I don't want to spoil our time together."

"You haven't. I appreciate that you care." She cupped his face and pressed her mouth to his.

And he did care for her. More than he could have expected in such a short time together. But he also knew it would be selfish to say as much when he didn't have a clue what should happen between them tomorrow, much less after he left the Top Dog Dude Ranch.

By the next afternoon, Eliza was stifling a yawn. But a night of making love with Nolan had been worth it. Even if she'd only gotten four hours of sleep.

The buzz of great sex, along with a double shot of espresso, was helping her get through the packed day.

Kneeling by her keyboard on the arena's corner stage, she unplugged the power, rehearsal complete. Thank goodness Nolan hadn't argued when she'd reminded him the hammock in her office was all his for the afternoon and that she would watch over Gus and Mavis. When he agreed, she tried to ignore the odd sense of relief that they would have the time apart. She needed to wrap her head around what had happened between them before they spent much more time together. While she had zero regrets, she also didn't have a clue how to handle whatever would happen next between them.

For band practice, they'd rehearsed with the children for the final presentation, which would include their production about the legend of

Sulis Springs. The songs were simple and all included animal themes, such as "Mary Had a Little Lamb" and "Old MacDonald." Afterward, they'd had lunch, consisting of wagon wheel–pasta macaroni and cheese along with "happy trails mix."

Now the children were napping in the tiny tents. Eliza waved goodbye to her other bandmates before picking her way around the little teepees, careful not to wake anyone but wanting to check on Gus and Mavis. A surreptitious peek reassured her the little girl was sleeping, thumb in her mouth. Cheese dotted her Yoda sweatshirt, and Eliza couldn't help but smile fondly.

Tiptoeing to the next canvas structure, she found Gus, sitting on his mat with a few books discarded beside him. He was scratching his arm, flecking away a temporary tattoo of bear tracks.

Eliza knelt in front of the opening and whispered, "Hey, kiddo, is there something I can help you with?"

Gus looked up and tucked his hands under his bottom. "When's Pop coming to get me?"

"He's resting, but he will be here soon." she assured him, only to be caught up short by the boy's crestfallen face. "Do you mind if I wait with you?"

"That would be good. I don't wanna be by myself, and Mavis is still sleeping." He looked up with wide eyes. "If you don't mind."

"I don't mind a bit. It's our job to look after you," she said as she sat cross-legged in front of the opening to his tent. "And even if it wasn't, I would still want to hang out with you. Is there something I can get for you? A snack?"

"Maybe at supper, I could have a purple cow? That's a grape juice with ice cream," he rushed to explain earnestly. "My daddy used to make that. Before he went to live in heaven. My mommy's there, too. I miss 'em." Gus averted his gaze, picking at the blanket in front of him. He swallowed before looking back up at Eliza. "Is it okay if I say that?"

Her heart squeezed inside her chest. "Of course it is." She searched for the right words to encompass such a big subject with a child. "My mom and dad are in heaven, too, and I miss them every day. You don't have to keep those feelings inside."

He shook his head, blond hair mussing. Picking at his flaking tattoo again, Gus took a deep breath. "I try not to say it in front of Pop because I don't want him to be sad. He's busy taking care of us, and he's probably sad, too."

"Of course he misses your parents. He loved

them just like he loves you and Mavis." Her mind raced back to that afternoon in Chattanooga, when she'd seen him for the first time, looking so very overwhelmed and, most of all, sad. "I bet he would like it if the two of you could talk about your parents together. It's good to remember the happy times."

Gus chewed his bottom lip for a second before nodding. "I think my mom and dad would like that. What did you like to do with your parents? To keep you from being sad?"

He patted her arm. The maturity of the gesture belied his years. Grief had a strange way of altering everyone—adults and children alike. Eliza looked up at the top of the canvas structure, desperate for the right explanation for what felt like an impossible question and subject.

And in that moment, she realized he wasn't just asking for himself but because he didn't want her to be upset. She swallowed a lump of emotion. The corners of her mouth threatened to go rogue, plummet into a frown in tandem with the tears that involuntarily lurked in the corners of her eyes. "We used to go to concerts in the park."

"What's that?" He scooted forward on his bottom until he sat beside her, head resting in his palms.

"A small band plays lots of songs, and people gather around to sit on the ground on blankets and listen to the music." The last one they'd attended—a Christmas concert—filled her memory with strains of carols and the taste of hot cocoa.

She could so easily slip back to that moment, to the glimmer of joy she saw in the faces of her parents—even though the weather that night had been fifteen degrees colder than the forecast. How her mom always belted along to the songs. Her dad, steadfast and serious, nodding in time to the chords. Heart swelling, a smile pushed gently on her mouth.

"Like Raise the Woof? With picnics?" He pointed to the sound stage still covered with instruments.

"What a smart boy you are." She tapped him on the nose, glad to see the sadness fading from his blue eyes that were so like his grandfather's. "In the winter, we always brought a thermos of hot cocoa. And in the summertime, we would pack pizza sandwiches and lemonade."

"What's a pizza sandwich?" He scrunched his nose.

"It's a sandwich with pepperoni, mozzarella cheese and a dab of pizza sauce, toasted until it's melted together." More smiles filled her at the recollection, and she realized the cutting sting of grief was finally losing its edge.

"Since Mavis can't eat cheese, maybe we could pack peanut butter and jelly for her. So we could go on a picnic, I mean." The little boy's words rolled out faster and faster. Bringing his hand to his chest, he pressed on. "I'll help you make the food. Pop usually has to cook, and I was thinking it might be fun for him to not have to for once. He's been really sad lately. Well, before we came here. I don't want him to be sad again when we get home."

His earnest face full of love and worry for his grandfather made her want to scoop Gus up and lift all those big burdens off his tiny shoulders.

"Of course, I'll teach you how to make pizza sandwiches," she said, unable to push more than a few words past the emotion clogging her throat and threatening to fill her eyes with tears.

"Thank you, Miss Eliza." Gus threw his arms around her waist and hugged her hard. "You're the best."

She hugged him back, grateful for the excuse to hide her face so he wouldn't see the tears in her eyes. This sweet, heartbroken kid was breaking her heart.

And for the first time, it hit her. Really sucker punched her deep in the gut. The Barnett family had been through so much already. They'd come to Top Dog Dude Ranch to heal their family from something truly traumatic. That healing was more important than any of the feelings she'd developed for Nolan. More important than the hurt she would feel when the week ended.

Because Gus's grief and his childish kindness had made her see that there could be no dabbling in a lighthearted, long-distance relationship with Nolan. This wasn't about just the two of them. These children had lost too much already. It was deeply unfair for her to insert herself into their lives if it was only going to be on a temporary basis.

The realization hurt, even though she knew for certain that her eyes were seeing things clearly now. She needed to end this brief fling with Nolan once and for all. Quickly. Quietly. Without upsetting the kids, who'd carved a place in her heart already.

No matter how tempted she was to make the most of Nolan's last days at the ranch, she would end things tonight.

Chapter Thirteen

Sitting on the edge of the hammock, his head in his hands, Nolan scrubbed his fingers through his hair, working to clear the sleep from his eyes. He'd napped, perhaps a little too deeply. So much so, when the alarm on his phone had woken him, his dreams had been jarring, too close to the surface. A tangle of the past and present. Memories of Heath as a child that morphed into Gus.

Memories of finding Rachel dying, only to roll her over to find Eliza.

He knew it wasn't rational. He would have liked a quick walk outside to clear his head, but he needed to collect the kids. He'd imposed on Eliza long enough.

He shoved to his feet, folded the fleece blanket, and tried not to think of how they'd made love on the sofa. The last thing he needed right now was another distraction.

Once he locked the door to Eliza's office, he pivoted toward the double doors connecting the stable to the arena. Only to stop short.

Eliza was standing by Cricket's stall with Gus and Mavis. Her ease with the children as she helped them feed the horse carrots took his breath away.

Cricket shook her head up and down, chomping on the carrot stick. Eliza handed a carrot to Mavis, showing her how to open her palm as she offered Cricket the treat. The horse sniffed Mavis's open palm, scooping the carrot up with a chuff and a lick. His granddaughter's laughter echoed in the barn, warming Nolan to his core. Gus tentatively stroked Cricket's muzzle as she crunched her latest snack. Nolan closed the distance, passing the other horses in the nearby stalls that lazily munched on hay.

As if she felt his gaze on her, Eliza tipped her head toward him, her eyes meeting his. He started to smile, only to be stopped short by the wariness in her eyes. By the distance in them that he'd never seen before.

What was wrong? He took a step closer.

She took a step back to the opening of Moonbeam's stall. The white mare popped her head out of the enclosure, clearly excited and anticipating treats. With a forceful headbutt, Moonbeam knocked into Eliza's shoulder. The impact was so great and so unexpected that Eliza stumbled, her feet slipping out from beneath her. Nolan felt like he watched her in slow motion fall backward and hit her head on one of the barn's wooden beams. Gus dropped the carrot from his hand. Both grandchildren screamed.

Seeing her fall knocked the air from Nolan's lungs, made his gut knot in fear, coming too close to the foggy remains of his nightmares. Forcing himself into doctor mode, he rushed to her side, calling out to the children, "Gus, Mavis, she's going to be fine. I need you to sit on your bottoms. Now."

He knew his voice was stern, but he couldn't risk them running around and getting hurt. Where was the rest of the stable staff?

As he knelt, Eliza was already trying to angle up. "Eliza, just be still for a minute. Let me check you over."

His tone came out sharper than he intended, his fear for her wrecking the composure he would bring to any other bedside situation.

"I'm fine." She brushed his hands away. "This isn't the first time I've been headbutted by a horse, and it certainly won't be the last."

"Humor me," he said grimly. Although by all accounts, her pulse was steadier than his.

At least her pupils were even and appropriately dilated for the light in the stables. He touched the bump on her forehead—red, but no split skin. In his peripheral vision, he caught sight of Jacob O'Brien with his son Elliot, both stepping up to the kids and reassuring them that Eliza was okay.

Jacob angled toward Nolan. "I'll take the kids over to the house. Take your time."

Nolan would have objected, but the children seemed eager to go with their new little friend. All the same, he reassured them, "I'll be there soon. I promise."

Eliza smiled, waving to the kids. "I'm fine. I promise. Your Pop will be right over."

Jacob's face was dark with concern as he gathered Mavis and Gus. He held each child's hand as they moved away. Even before he was out of earshot, Gus started firing a million questions about head injuries to the Top Dog owner.

Nolan was grateful to be able to focus solely on Eliza. To make sure she was all right. And yes, to reassure himself, too.

But his patient was already pushing to her feet, bracing a hand against a beam. "I'm really okay. Moonbeam just caught me by surprise. My pride's bruised far more than my head. I just hate that it scared the children."

"They seemed to be okay once they saw you sit up." He, on the other hand, was still struggling.

Eliza tipped her head to the side, studying him through narrowed eyes. "Are *you* all right? Maybe we should go to my office and talk."

The last thing he wanted—or needed—right now was to return to a place where his thoughts had gotten so tangled. Maybe it would help if he explained the reason for his reaction—but not yet. He needed to get away from here first. "If you're feeling up to it, let's walk outside, clear our heads. Then I can head straight over to get the children."

"I'd like that." Her throat moving in a long swallow, she stuffed her hands into her parka pockets. "I have something I need to speak with you about as well."

Nolan opened the barn door, and they stepped out from the relative warmth of the barn to a biting cold. The sun was dipping behind the mountain, lights beginning to flicker on. A handful of guests strolled toward the dining hall; others were heading in the direction of their cabins.

Drawing in a bracing breath of fresh air, he gestured to a wooden bench by the firepit, the stoned ring large enough to provide them with privacy from the two people sitting on the other side. The flames licked high toward the darkening sky, adding an additional layer of seclusion along with warmth. "I want to apologize for my reaction back in the barn when you were hurt. It was over the top and unprofessional."

She flattened her gloved hands to the wooden bench. "You were worried. That's understandable. And I wouldn't call your response *unprofessional* in the least. You were quick to act."

"While I appreciate you attempting to let me off the hook, I need you to understand. When I was sleeping, I had some pretty vivid nightmares about Rachel… my wife. About her death." He wasn't in any state to admit that Eliza had been in those dreams as well, especially when he still hadn't sorted through what it all meant. "Those were still close to the surface when I saw you get hurt."

"I see," she said, shadows in her eyes as her hands turned to fists on the bench.

"Her aneurysm was quick." He took a beat to steady his breathing, staring at his booted feet on the stony ground to keep from staring at the bump on Eliza's forehead. "I take comfort in that much, at least. It was harder for our son, though. He was angry over not being able to say goodbye."

"I'm so sorry." Her hand slid over his on his knee.

"It's been five years. I'm moving on. I just wanted you to understand." He looked up at her, wondering what it was about this woman that had opened the vault of things he'd never shared with anyone else. "And now that I have that out of the way, what did you want to talk to me about?"

He remembered her expression from earlier, before she'd fallen. He recalled the wariness. The distance.

But maybe he'd misinterpreted her, given the fog he'd been in. He sure hoped so. Right now, he found it tough to read her eyes as she gazed into the fire.

"I was talking with Gus earlier," she began slowly. "The others were napping, and he didn't want to be alone."

"I appreciate you spending that extra time with him. The kids have really enjoyed getting to know you."

Another wary glance his way. He knew for sure he hadn't misinterpreted this one.

"I've enjoyed being with them, too, Nolan. They're great kids. And I know it may sound obvious, but when I was sitting with Gus in the tent, I really saw what he's going through. I realized how much he needs you."

He cursed lowly under his breath. His disappointment crackling through him as insistently as the firepit's flame. "I should have been there. Thank you for sitting with him."

She wrapped her arms around herself, exhaling as she leaned closer to the firepit. "I don't say this to make you feel bad. I feel guilty enough for having taken you away from him for our time together when you made it clear your trip to the ranch was about the children."

"What are you trying to say?" He sensed the tenor of the conversation, but he didn't want to believe it. Despite the warmth of the fire, Nolan felt cold sweep through him.

She unwrapped her arms, closing her eyes for a moment. Seeming to collect herself.

"I've enjoyed our time together, so very much."

In a fluid movement, her hands cupped his cheeks, eyes bright in the flamelight. "But there's no future for us. Not even in the time you have left here."

Even as he knew deep in his gut that she was right, he didn't want it to be true. Every cell in him shouted for them to find a compromise. Not to give up. There had to be a solution. He clasped her wrists, keeping her touch against his face. "How can you be so sure? What if we tried long distance? Chattanooga may be a haul to commute, but it's not the edge of the universe."

"It might as well be." Eliza eased her hands to his shoulder. "I deeply admire how committed you are to Gus and Mavis, and it's clear how much they need you right now. They have to come first—and they should. We've barely been able to make time for each other here. What makes you think we can pull off a long-distance romance?"

Her logic knocked around inside him, swelling until it squeezed his heart painfully. The thought of losing her, losing the feelings they'd just begun to explore with each other, hurt. More than he could have imagined, given the short time they'd known each other.

But even as he wanted to argue with her, to

fight for what they had, she was right. His responsibility to the children had to come first.

So he sighed in surrender, his forehead falling to rest against hers as he whispered, "I wish you were wrong. God, how I wish it."

Embers from the firepit floated skyward, trapped in the hazy smoke. Like the end of their relationship?

Nolan stroked back her hair, taking in the beauty of her one last time. She pressed her mouth to his, holding, in a clear farewell that tore him up inside, no matter how much he told himself that this was for the best. There was no way for them to be together. His grandchildren needed him.

And Eliza deserved her chance to pursue her dreams. He cared about her too much to hold her back or ask her to compromise on her dreams.

He'd been through a lot in his life, lost more than most. So much so, he'd thought he was impervious to whatever blows life might have left in store for him. But right now, watching Eliza walk out of his life threatened to drive him to his knees.

Declan stretched his feet in front of him, the terra-cotta chiminea on Charlotte's patio radiating heat into the early evening. But somehow it didn't chase away the chill in his gut over what he had to tell Charlotte. It didn't help that she was looking far too appealing in her bright pink parka and blond braids. She was such a natural beauty.

Their relationship was still so new he didn't know how she would react. Especially since she'd been acting distant and distracted from the moment Rory's text had come in during their night at the springs. He wanted to believe her new reserve was his imagination, but he'd been a cop too long to ignore his instincts.

"Thank you for coming over." Charlotte leaned forward in her chair, holding her gloved hands closer to the fire, her every gesture twitchy and nervous. "I don't want to risk leaving Rory alone, not after his last stunt."

"I'm just glad he's okay." Declan had seen too much—done too much in his own youth—not to be concerned for the boy. Which meant he worried about Charlotte as well and the challenges she faced in handling a troubled teen.

"I appreciate your understanding." Her blue eyes filled with gratitude that almost pushed away the deep sadness he could see lurking there. A kindling stick in hand, she swirled the melting snow around the terra-cotta chiminea.

"I need you to know I really enjoyed our time together in the cave, and I don't regret making love with you, not for a moment…"

He went stone-still, all his instincts cranking on high alert, telling him something bad was coming. "But?"

"But I think we should take a break," she said quickly, wrapping her arms around herself, her hands rubbing along her sleeves. "The timing of this is all wrong with my brother moving here. He's not a bad kid—there's just so much baggage with our parents that he needs to deal with… I have to focus all my attention on making sure he's on the right path."

She eyed him warily, silently, as she leaned forward in her Adirondack chair.

Frustration seared through him because being with Charlotte had been incredible, and not just the sex. She was a funny, smart woman, and he didn't want to let her go. But he had to—because she was right.

Rory needed her.

Declan's eyes flicked to her log cabin and the warm glow of the lights pouring out the window. Declan could make out Rory's head in the shadows, angled toward the TV.

The kid was a ticking time bomb, and the

window of time to defuse him was short. Knowing and accepting that made it simpler for him to tell her… "I, uh, got some news today. I'm being called up. National Guard duty."

Her forehead furrowed. "Your regular weekend training?"

Drumming his fingers on the arm of his chair, he stared hard at anything but her. The heat of the chiminea decimated the surrounding snow, leaving a mess.

"No. Longer than that. I'm being activated."

Standing, she circled over to him, sitting on the edge of his chair. "Where? For how long?"

The worry stamped all over her face only amplified his resolve that he needed to let her go. He couldn't add more burdens to her already-overloaded life.

Declan surveyed the grounds, trying to soak in all the details of this place—the spilt-rail fence, the perfectly decorated garden, the amazing woman right in front of him. "The specifics haven't been confirmed yet, but I know it will be soon. It feels like a sign, given what you just said." Rising, he took her hands in his and pulled her up with him. "I've enjoyed our time together these past couple of weeks. You're an incredible lady, but it's over."

"Wait," she said, squeezing his fingers, her cheeks rosy from the wind, as pink as her parka. "I know what I said earlier, but…if you have an address, I'll write."

He appreciated her big heart, the way she couldn't let him leave for military duty with a fresh breakup.

It said a lot about her.

And maybe that was just one more reason why he needed to accept that they couldn't be together.

"No," he said firmly, telling himself it was for the best. "We've had a fling, and it's over. I'm not a white-picket-fence kind of guy. This is goodbye."

Eliza blinked back tears as she put distance between herself and Nolan as quickly as she could without slipping on the ice. She didn't even know exactly where she was going—just taking one step at a time through the snow away from him.

Her heart was broken. Truly broken. Far more than from any breakup in her past, even from relationships that had lasted for years. It didn't make sense. But then, love didn't make sense.

Love? She shied away from the word that would only make her pain worse.

In a daze, she walked, tears icing on her cheeks until she ended up exactly where she needed to be. On a friend's doorstep. As she started up the steps to Charlotte Pace's cabin, Eliza caught sight of the woman in the side yard, sitting alone by a flaming chiminea. Charlotte's pink parka was a splash of color in an otherwise shadowy evening as murky as her mood.

Backing up, Eliza walked past a fat oak with a sign hanging from one of the glistening branches: "Life's a Garden. Dig It."

If only things could be that easy. Drawing in a breath of cold air that seemed to crystalize shards inside her, Eliza tapped on the fence in a knock of sorts. "Hello? Are you up for some unexpected company?"

Because she desperately needed a friend.

Charlotte jolted, as if startled from a daze, then shot to her feet. "Eliza, what's going on? You look upset."

"Man troubles," she said, struggling to keep her chin from quivering. "I've ruined everything with Nolan, and I don't have a clue what to do."

"Oh, hon, it's a great big ditto from me on the man troubles." Charlotte pulled her close and hugged her hard before angling back. "Do you want to come inside? I have ice cream and tissues and nowhere else to be."

Nodding, Eliza scrubbed her sleeve across her

gritty eyes. "That sounds like the best offer I've had in a long time."

She didn't hold out hope on any quick fix to her broken heart, but at least she wouldn't be alone.

Chapter Fourteen

Nolan usually found comfort in staying busying, appreciating the oblivion brought by activity.

Too bad that wasn't working to ease his misery since the breakup with Eliza. The hurt, the loss left him sleepless and empty inside. Knowing she was right about the need to separate gave him zero comfort. He hadn't realized how deeply lonely he'd been until she'd entered his life—and now, contemplating going forward without her... the ache was far deeper than he ever would have imagined. But he just had to get through the next twenty-four hours until it was time to pack up the kids and head home.

Nolan stood by the massive farmhouse sink in the cabin, with Gus sitting on the kitchen counter beside him while Mavis napped. The boy was holding a wet paper towel against Nolan's hand, insisting his grandfather wear a temporary tattoo as well.

Nolan didn't have the heart—or energy—to argue.

The boy already had seven, all dog themed, on his arms, hands and a cheek. But Gus had insisted on more, claiming he needed them for his big performance this evening. He'd been cast in the role of a puppy in the play about the legend of Sulis Springs. Gus vowed that he was the star. Nolan appreciated that the staff had helped the boy understand his role as "the puppy" was crucial. After all, the place was called the Top *Dog* Dude Ranch.

Once the theater production was over, there would be a family-friendly dinner party before bed. When the sun came up, his time here at the Top Dog Dude Ranch would be finished. Done. Over. No more painful encounters with Eliza—on a horse, in the dining hall, walking Loki. Every glimpse of her poured alcohol on the wound left by their breakup.

Gus eased back the paper towel on Nolan's

hand to peek at the temporary tattoo's progress, then pressed it down again to keep transferring the ink. "I really like it here at the ranch."

At least the trip had helped his grandkids as he'd hoped. Certainly he felt he'd come a long way in caring for them since that first day when he'd been hit in the head with a sippy cup. Spending this precious time with them had given him memories he would always treasure. "I'm glad you had fun making s'mores and roasting hotdogs over the campfire today, buddy."

"I've made lots of new friends." Gus swung his legs, his feet in horse-print socks thumping against the cabinets softly. "I'm gonna miss them when we go home."

Nolan didn't want to think about the hole in his life from leaving Eliza behind. "I bet they're going to miss you when they go home, too."

Shaking his head, Gus sighed. "No, I mean that I'm gonna miss my friends who *live* here. Like Benji—his dad builds stuff here. And Elliot and Phillip—their mom and dad run the place." His feet still thudding against the cabinets, Gus set aside the paper towel and peeled off the plastic, revealing the red paw print on Nolan's hand. A grin spread across Gus's face, eyes wide and dancing with satisfaction at his handiwork. "Then there are the triplets. Their mama runs the gift shop with all the great toys."

"That's a lot of new pals." Nolan couldn't help but think of the people he'd met since coming here other than Eliza—Declan, Charlotte, the O'Briens, just to name a few. He'd been welcomed—befriended, even.

"You know what, though? I'm gonna miss Miss Eliza most." Gus's legs went still, and he rubbed a palm over the Top Dog logo on his sweatshirt. "I wish we could live here all the time."

His grandson's words were like a sucker punch to Nolan's gut. As if he wasn't already hauling around enough guilt for all the boy was missing out on in life. "I'm sorry, but we already have a home, and I have to get back to my job."

Gus tipped his head to the side, his blue eyes earnest. "Why can't you work here like their mommies and daddies do? There are sick kids for you to take care of in Moonlight Ridge, too."

"Because—" Nolan began, but then stopped himself. Three weeks ago, he would have answered on autopilot, explaining why he couldn't possibly upend their lives.

But sometime during these last two weeks, he'd quit going through the motions. He'd started paying attention. Tuning in. Operating on a slower frequency. Really thinking about questions instead of just giving a pat answer.

So now Nolan blinked, rendered speechless at the boy's simple—on-point—logic.

Could it really be that easy? Relocate to Moonlight Ridge? Step off the workaholic hamster wheel that had robbed him of so much time with his family and embrace a simpler existence here?

For his whole life, he'd bought into the plan of continuing the family practice. But had that just become a way to hang on to the past? Because somehow, that kept a semblance of ties to Rachel and their son? He had to admit to himself that there was a real possibility it was exactly that.

Tucking his hands under Gus's arms, Nolan lifted him off the counter. "That's a good idea I haven't thought about before—but right now, we need to finish getting ready for the play."

As he ushered Gus toward the bedroom where his costume was laid out, Nolan wondered if his definition of legacy needed to be retooled. To his way of thinking, the best way to honor the past was to live life to the fullest. To focus on the future, on these children and his feelings for Eliza.

Was it possible he could still have a chance with her?

He sifted through what he and Eliza had said to

each other when they'd broken off their relationship. None of it had anything to do with a lack of feelings for one another. Just the opposite, in fact. And they'd built that relationship while juggling their everyday lives. The connection between them was so strong it tore them up inside to split.

The biggest obstacle to them being together? Distance.

It truly was that simple to overcome if he wanted to win her back. Which he did. More than he'd even allowed himself to consider until this moment.

Because he'd fallen in love with Eliza.

Even though they'd only known each other for a brief time, there was no doubt. He wasn't a green youth. He was a man who knew his mind; he knew his heart. And his heart belonged to Eliza.

Hadn't he learned that life was too short to pass up the chance for love? For happiness?

Whatever it took, he was going to make a move to Moonlight Ridge happen—for the children, for himself, for the hope of a future with Eliza.

Hands poised over the keyboard, Eliza struggled to stay focused on the children's performance of songs, poems and local dances, concluding with a brief play acting out the legend of Sulis Springs. The last thing she needed was to let her horrible mood and broken heart somehow tarnish this precious production.

The kids all wore jeans and Top Dog Dude Ranch sweatshirts, with costume add-ons of different animal ears and painted faces. The toddlers sat on a blanket with Hollie, the tiny tots looking adorable in gnome hats. Mavis waved to her grandfather, then at Eliza, blowing a heart-tugging kiss.

If only she could keep her eyes off Nolan, looking too handsome sitting on the bleachers with the other families and guests. If only she could keep herself from thinking about him leaving tomorrow morning. Her throat went tight at the thought of never seeing him or his grandchildren again. How had the three of them become so dear to her in such a brief time?

With a shaky hand, she turned the page on her sheet music, grounding herself in the sights and sounds around her. Sweet young voices filled the arena, accompanied by Raise the Woof, with Eliza on the keyboard.

Rainbow colors brought the mural scene on the canvas to life. Hanging on the arena wall, the mural captured the surreal beauty of the local woods. The large canvas hung behind the risers where all the children were standing and depicted a cave in the middle of a forest. Basic scenery had been outlined in bold black lines, and the children had filled in the rest with vibrant colors.

A box of props sat to one side of the risers by the rocking chair, where librarian Susanna Levine narrated from an oversize storybook, a scruffy little dog curled up on her lap.

The band was tucked to the other side— keyboard, guitar, banjo and fiddle. Older children played the spoons, washboard, metal washtub and more. One even blew into a big jug.

As the children's latest musical number drew to a close, Susanna began, "The magical history of our corner of the mountain began hundreds of years ago, when the O'Brien ancestors were settling into this area. One day, they went walking in the woods and began to follow a very special doe…" She paused as a row of children filed out to follow a child with antlers. "And the doe transformed into the Queen of the Forest."

A seven-year-old girl with bouncing ringlets pulled wings and a floral crown from the costume box and pirouetted as Susanna continued, "She glowed like starlight. Now, the O'Briens were from Scotland and Ireland, so they knew the Queen of the Forest used to roam Scotland and lead wayward souls to safe places and healing water."

As a tinkling waterfall of notes flowed from Eliza's fingertips on the keyboard, the story played out in front of her in sweet simplicity. It was more than a legend, more than a simple tale. Every day working here, she saw the way the healing nature of this place transformed people's lives. And while it hadn't brought her the ending she'd hoped for with Nolan, she took comfort in seeing the strengthened bond between him and those two children, who'd worked their way into her heart too. And in some far corner of her soul, she couldn't help but wonder if the ranch had a miracle to pull out for her as well.

Susanna's voice pierced Eliza's thoughts as the narrator leaned forward in her rocker. "Okay, so this next part is important because those long ago O'Briens were having a tough time settling into this region. They even wanted to give up on the land. And on each other. But they followed the Queen of the Forest to a cave, where they found a puppy, lost and dirty and cold."

Gus leapt from the risers, wearing a baseball cap with long dog ears. He plopped onto his bottom and shivered with exaggerated intensity, drawing a sympathetic *aww* from the crowd. Eliza couldn't help but slip a peek at Nolan, his proud smile stirring butterflies in her stomach.

Susanna waited for a trio of children to lead Gus to a large metal washtub. "They cleaned up the young pup. As they rinsed the puppy together, they found their connection was back. Their love was healed."

The crowd cheered and Gus broke into an impromptu happy dance that drew chuckles from the adults. Once the crowd settled, the play resumed as Susanna motioned for each of the children to follow one another in a winding path. "Since then, people take the same path back to the cave that houses Sulis Springs. They leave pumpkins and fresh-cut sunflowers for the Queen of the Forest in thanks for her magic that brings people together."

The children reached under their bleachers and picked up tiny baskets full of dried flowers and flower petals, tossing the blooms forward in a shower of fragrant color. Applause and cheers filled the arena, the audience rising to their feet in a resounding standing ovation for the young performers. Two children from the play high-fived each other nearby.

Unable to withstand another moment when

her heart was so heavy, Eliza turned off the power to the keyboard and moved to make her escape off the back of the low stage. She needed to sneak away to cry her eyes out.

Her booted feet hit the dirt, but she didn't have a chance to escape because she found herself immediately face-to-face with Nolan, holding Mavis in her gnome hat on his hip. Gus, with his puppy ears, stood by Nolan's side. Each child held a bouquet of a dozen roses.

She swallowed a lump and plastered a smile on her face. "Congratulations on doing such a good job out there." She touched each child gently on the cheek. "Your flowers are lovely."

Gus stepped forward, extending the red roses clutched in his hands. "These are for you."

Mavis held hers out as well—pink flowers tied with a lacy white bow. "For you."

Eliza looked to Nolan, and he nodded, easing Mavis to the ground and passing over the bouquet. Both children wrapped their arms tight around her, and she knelt to hug them back, close, her eyes stinging. Through the haze of tears, she saw other families hugging each other, laughing. It all seemed so simple for everyone else. But it was different for her. Saying goodbye to these kids and Nolan? Tears continued to well as her jaw tightened.

Gus whispered in her ear, "Love you, Miss Eliza."

Mavis kissed Eliza on the cheek before both children backed away.

The little boy grinned. "We're going to a party with Ms. Hollie and Mr. Jacob and their kids. Bye-bye."

Already her arms ached as they each clasped hands with the O'Briens and faded into the crowd. Even full of flowers, Eliza's arms felt so empty.

People milled about, chattering as they discussed plans for their next pack-tivities. And just like that, her life would return to the routine of work and nothing more.

Nolan extended a hand, cupping her elbow to help her stand. A temporary tattoo of a paw print was inked on his hand. No doubt at Gus's request.

Lordy, she loved this incredible man. She hadn't been prepared for this last kindness. Her throat closed up, and she had to clear it before she spoke. "Thank you. For the flowers and for bringing the children to say goodbye. That's so very thoughtful." She tapped his hand. "Nice tattoo."

He smiled sheepishly. "Gus insisted the paw print would be good luck for the production."

What did the flowers mean? "Well, uh, I should let you get back to the children."

"They've made it quite clear they want to party with their friends. I'll join them shortly."

"What's this all about?" She lifted the flowers slightly. Because as much as she ached to see him, she also wasn't interested in having her emotions put through a cheese grater yet again.

Nolan shifted from foot to foot, as if nervous. "Can you break away for a few minutes? I have something important to speak with you about."

That whisper of hope she'd felt earlier returned. Grew stronger. "Sure." She considered suggesting they go to her office, but there were too many memories there. "We can talk in the stables."

Shoulders almost brushing, they moved through the dispersing crowd. People bottlenecked at the doors, and Eliza had to stop so abruptly she nearly tripped over the threshold. His hand had been there to steady her. The slight touch drew forth an intoxicating mix of hope and despair. Increasing her stride, she led them toward the stables and opened the double doors.

With each step, she was all too aware of his strong presence behind her. Guiding them through the heart of the barn, she did her best to steady her erratic breathing. Eliza stopped walking once she reached the far corner, where Cricket poked her head out of the stall, greeting them with a nicker. Setting the flowers aside, on an up-side-down water bucket, she turned to face him.

Her chest went tight, and her pulse leapt wildly. A thousand questions piled up inside her, but she wanted—needed—to hear whatever was on his mind first.

"I hate how we left things the other day." His blue eyes darkened with pain, his hand in a fist on the edge of the stall door. "Every minute without you has been torture."

"I've missed you, too, so much," she admitted, even though it didn't solve a thing. Eliza picked a piece of hay out of Cricket's mane, twirling it between her thumb and index finger. "I'm so sorry if I hurt you. I was so upset after the con-versation with Gus…"

He drew in a shuddering sigh, his fist unfurl-ing to grip the stall. "You have nothing to apolo-gize for. You care about my grandson's welfare, and that means the world to me. I came a little unhinged when you hit your head. I made it too easy to push me away. And that's a mistake I want to rectify."

She could barely believe her ears. She tried to swallow down her excitement, not wanting to presume only to get hurt again. She sucked in a deep breath, the earthy scents of well-worn leather calming her. "What do you mean?"

He skimmed her hair from her face, his hands traveling to palm the small of her back. "Eliza Hubbard, I love you. With all my heart and soul. More than anything, I want the chance to win your love in return. So I'm moving to Moonlight Ridge."

A beat passed as she tried to make sense of what he'd said. Her heart had started hammering when he'd mentioned love, the pulsing so loud she'd almost missed that last bit about him...relocating?

"What?" she could barely push the word past the shock. "You're moving? I don't understand. You have a practice you've worked so hard at."

His expression was calm and certain. Clear-eyed.

"I'm hanging up my shingle here because I can practice medicine anywhere—as Gus so aptly pointed out earlier today."

Gus again. She had to smile at the thought of a four-year-old's wisdom.

It sounded perfect, like a dream come true. Still, she had to know, "What about your medical practice with your father?"

"My father and I already had a conversation

about it this morning. And while he isn't thrilled, he also accepts that this isn't about him. This is about my life, about Gus and Mavis's future. And we believe in the healing magic of this place. More importantly, we hope you'll let us be a part of your life. Because, Eliza, I know it's fast, but I'm a man who knows his own heart. I know what love feels like. And I've fallen deeply, irrevocably in love with you."

Tears of joy filled her eyes, and she threw her arms around his neck. Cricket nudged her arm, clearly not wanting to miss this moment. "Nolan, I love you, too, so very much. I can't believe you're doing this for me. For us."

"I would do anything for you," he whispered against her mouth, holding her tight, sealing his lips to hers for a heartfelt second that relayed just how afraid he'd been. "I want to have the time to show you. I don't want to waste our opportunities to be together with commuting. There's nothing I want more than to romance you, to sweep you off your feet." Nolan held her arms gently, all his love for her right there in his eyes. "How does that sound to you?"

As Eliza reveled in the beautiful moment, committing every nuance to memory, Cricket nudged her on the shoulder, gently, urging her closer to

Nolan, and Eliza couldn't help but remember that first time she'd seen him. How, thanks to another furry friend, they'd landed in each other's paths.

Eliza leaned against Nolan's chest, her mouth a whisper away from his. "The cowgirl and the country MD? I think that sounds like a match made in heaven."

* * * * *

For more delightful holiday romance, check out these other great books from Harlequin Special Edition:

The Marine's Christmas Wish
By Joanna Sims
The Cowboy's Christmas Retreat
By Catherine Mann
Sleigh Ride with the Rancher
By Stella Bagwell

Available now wherever Harlequin Special Edition books and ebooks are sold!

**WE HOPE YOU ENJOYED
THIS BOOK FROM**

**SPECIAL
EDITION**

Believe in love. Overcome obstacles. Find happiness.

Relate to finding comfort and strength in the
support of loved ones and enjoy the journey
no matter what life throws your way.

6 NEW BOOKS AVAILABLE EVERY MONTH!

So that was an option, just to say that she needed her alone
time and West would intrude on that. Everyone would
understand. But then he would stay at the Heartwood Inn
and that really wasn't right…

And what about just telling everyone that it would be
awkward because she and West had shared a one-night
stand? There was nothing unacceptable about what she
and West had done. No one here would judge her. Alex
and West were both adults, both single. It was nobody's
business that they'd had sex on a cold winter night when
he'd needed a friend and she was the only one around
to hold out a hand. It was one of those things that just
happen sometimes.

It would be weird, though, to share that information
with the family. Weird and awkward. And Alex still
hoped she would never have to go there.

"Alex?" Weston spoke again, his voice so smooth and deep and way too sexy.

"Hmm?"

"You ever plan on answering my question?"

"Absolutely." It came out sounding aggressive, almost angry. She made herself speak more cordially. "Yes. Honestly. There's plenty of room here. You're staying in the cottage. It's settled."

"You're so bossy…" He said that kind of slowly—slowly and also naughtily—and she sincerely hoped her cheeks weren't cherry red.

"Weston." She said his name sternly as a rebuke.

"Alexandra," he mocked.

"That's a yes, right?" Now she made her voice pleasant, even a little too sweet. "You'll take the second bedroom."

"Yes, I will. And it's good to talk to you, Alex. At last." Did he really have to be so…ironic? It wasn't like she hadn't thought more than once of reaching out to him, checking in with him to see how he was holding up. But back in January, when they'd said goodbye, he'd seemed totally on board with cutting it clean. "Alex? You still there?"

"Uh, yes. Great."

"See you day after tomorrow. I'll be flying down with Easton."

"Perfect. See you then." She heard the click as he disconnected the call.

Don't miss
The Christmas Cottage *by Christine Rimmer,*
available November 2022 wherever
Harlequin Special Edition books and ebooks are sold.

Harlequin.com

Get 4 FREE REWARDS!

We'll send you 2 FREE Books <u>plus</u> 2 FREE Mystery Gifts.

FREE
Value Over
$20

Both the **Harlequin® Special Edition** and **Harlequin® Heartwarming™** series feature compelling novels filled with stories of love and strength where the bonds of friendship, family and community unite.

HARLEQUIN
PLUS

Announcing a **BRAND-NEW** multimedia subscription service for romance fans like you!

Read, Watch and Play.

Experience the easiest way to get the romance content you crave.

Start your **FREE 7 DAY TRIAL** at
www.harlequinplus.com/freetrial.

HARLEQUIN

Heartfelt or thrilling, passionate or uplifting—Harlequin is more than just happily-ever-after.

With twelve different series to choose from and new books available every month, you are sure to find stories that will move you, uplift you, inspire and delight you.

Love Harlequin romance?

DISCOVER.

Be the first to find out about promotions, news and exclusive content!

f Facebook.com/HarlequinBooks

🐦 Twitter.com/HarlequinBooks

📷 Instagram.com/HarlequinBooks

📌 Pinterest.com/HarlequinBooks

You Tube YouTube.com/HarlequinBooks

ReaderService.com

EXPLORE.

Sign up for the Harlequin e-newsletter and download a free book from any series at **TryHarlequin.com**

CONNECT.

Join our Harlequin community to share your thoughts and connect with other romance readers!
Facebook.com/groups/HarlequinConnection

HSOCIAL2021